The Shadow-man

By

C.S. Marks

The Shadow-man

The characters and events this book are entirely fictional. No similarity between any of the names, characters, persons, and/or institutions in this book with those of any living or dead person or institutions is intended, and any such similarity which may exist is purely coincidental.

Copyright © 2014 by C. S. Marks, Iron Elf, LLC

All rights reserved. No part of this book may be reproduced in any form by any electronic or mechanical means including photo- copying, recording, or information storage and retrieval without permission in writing from the author.

Cover art by John Connell

Published by Parthian Press, all rights reserved

ParthianPress.com
ISBN: 978-0-9912351-1-7

FOREWORD

Welcome to the third offering in the *Alterra Histories* series of novellas.

In case you're unfamiliar with them, they are the result of my attempting to expand on some of the characters and events alluded to in the *Elfhunter* trilogy, a series of three books set in the fantasy world of Alterra. They're relatively brief, stand-alone ventures, affording fans a bit of additional insight into some of their favorite characters. They also provide new readers with an introduction to my world and writing style.

I choose the subject matter for the novellas based on reader curiosity (influenced mightily by my own desire to shed more light on a particular character). The first two novellas, *The Fire King* and *Fallen Embers*, tell the stories of Aincor Fire-heart and Ri-Elathan, respectively. They are set in Elven realms, and therefore have a certain "loftiness" about them.

Shadow-man is different, being entirely devoid of Elves. Here we travel to the south and east into the desert realms of Men, straight into the personal history of one of the more intriguing minor characters in the series.

Readers have been asking about him since the first publication of *Fire-heart* (the second book in the *Elfhunter* trilogy). I can't say I blame them...I mean, who can resist the mysterious character with a shadowed past? There's something about him that makes you want to know more, especially after he reappears in the third book, *Ravenshade*.

There's nothing "lofty" in *Shadow-man*. It begins during the Plague years--a time filled with terror, madness, and despair. It's a grittier, more graphic offering--a depiction of the struggle to remain human--of survival in the face of the unspeakable. Such events shape everyone touched by them. This is the story of one...

—CSM

The Shadow-Man

I killed my first man when I was eleven. No doubt he would have died anyway, but I most certainly hastened his end. Our father had taught us never to do such a thing—that killing was wrong—but he was gone. He was gone, and I couldn't worry about what was right or wrong.

It hadn't always been that way. If I try hard enough, I can still remember summer days with my family, cookfires, times of hard work and hard play, guiding words and comforting hands. Then everything went mad. Everything went mad, and I became a man at the age of eleven, or so I thought at the time. I had no idea of what "becoming a man" was really about.

It started with a caravan of merchants, which was an ordinary enough occurrence and usually celebrated, as it meant new and wondrous items to be purchased. My father, who was in desperate need of a new hand-axe, purchased a good one. Finely tempered and polished, it would have served him well for many years, but he only used it a few times. It hangs from my belt now.

I remember clamoring for a sight of the caravan and its wares, begging to be allowed a few coins to spend, but my father said none could be spared. He reminded me, as he often did, of the difference between "want" and "need."

I knew things weren't right when I overheard my mother urging him to avoid the people of the caravan, as if there was something unwholesome about them. "There's something wrong with them," she had said. "There's a shadow over their souls." If only he had listened…but I suppose it was too late by then, anyway. The shadow was already among us.

I had my first taste of it on the heels of what I thought was good fortune. I had found a coin in the dust—an old, tarnished copper, hardly worth anything. I thought perhaps I could buy a sweet, which, since no one else knew I had found the coin, I wouldn't be compelled to share with my brother and sister. I crept to the merchants' tent and peered inside.

It smelled bad, and the hair on the back of my neck stood straight up, but my new-found wealth was crying to be spent.

"Hello?"

I looked deeper into the dim confines of the tent, breathing in the swirling blue smoke that drifted everywhere. It smelled sweet, but it couldn't mask the stench pervading the air. I hadn't ever encountered it before. The closest I could recall was that of a newly-dead carcass, just beginning to rot. The blowflies would have come, and the maggots would already be at work.

A man grabbed the back of my neck, and I squealed, startled, as he spun me around. His face—his eyes—I will never forget them. "Get away from here, boy! Get away if you want to live!" He literally flung me out of the tent, an act which seemed to elicit a terrible fit of coughing. He doubled over, coughing so hard that blood ran down his chin and into his beard. I needed nothing else to convince me, and I ran away as fast as I could. I only saw him once after that—amid the bodies of the dead.

By the time we realized how terribly sick the merchantmen were, the seeds of death had already been sown. Anyone who had contacted them directly would be the first to suffer...all except father and me. Our mother fell ill after visiting one of the other families, every one of whom had been laid low. She brought their youngest child—a babe in arms—into our tent, weeping as she held her. "She is alone now. All the others are dead." My mother was a gentle spirit.

Needless to say, the little one did not live long, blue and gasping as its tiny lungs filled up with blood. Well, perhaps not needless to say, as it soon became clear that some of our folk did not get the Sickness. Others sickened but did not die—not at first. My mother was among them. She recovered, but it left her so damaged that we wondered whether she would ever be herself again. When the scourge had burned its way through our little settlement, only a few remained alive and unmarked. We did not yet realize what that would mean.

Most of our sheep and goats had also sickened and died. The few that survived, like my mother, were left with terrible damage. They wandered, witless and half-blind, through the empty tents. Their flesh fell away, for they would not eat, and their milk dried up. I found a healthy kid, bleating beside his dead mother, but I had nothing to feed him.

Mother was just like the sheep, half blind and witless, her face covered with sores that would not heal. Father tried to help her, but she would not eat, and she soon passed away in the night. I heard my father weeping, and in the morning she was gone—I never saw her again. Father had gathered the last few bodies of the dead, and he set them afire in the early morning light. He stood with my brother Seth, my sister Salina, and me, watching the smoke billowing toward heaven, praying that our mother would find her eternal home.

***

We had plenty of provisions left behind by the dead. Once we had burned all the bodies, the settlement was livable, but we saw the ghosts of our friends and neighbors everywhere. The empty tents and market-stalls were never silent—it was as though we could hear voices carried in the wind. Father tried to be strong, but he wept every night. I wept, too, and I felt more guilt than a boy of eleven should ever have to—if only I hadn't found that penny and gone into the merchants' tent, the Sickness might have spared us.

One day our father left us, promising to return as soon as he could manage. "I'm going to see if I can find other survivors. We can't stay alone forever," he said. Then he knelt down in front of me, looked me straight in the eye, and placed both hands on my shoulders. "Glennroy, as the eldest, you must take care of our family until I return." He gave me his new hand-axe. "If enemies threaten, stay hidden. If they find you, use this if you can't run away."

I nodded, solemn-faced, as he smiled down at me. "I know you can keep our family safe, my son. Take care of Seth and Salina." Then he was gone.

Days passed, nights came and went, and we made our way as best we could. We ate and drank, played games and told stories, but we were afraid, especially at night. Though we always built a fire, the darkness seemed to close in around us as we huddled together. Then, one night, we heard voices—real voices, not ghost-voices—and I knew we had been found.

Several rough-looking men came upon our campfire, intent on taking whatever they could find of value. We had gone into hiding by then, but they knew we were there. "Find whoever made this fire, and we'll soon learn where they keep their valuables," said one. "We'll have some sport tonight!" As he turned toward me in the fire-light, I saw his face—the telltale scarring—and I knew he had once had the Sickness. His eyes betrayed the madness it had left behind.

I clutched my father's axe with both hands, knowing that I wouldn't stand a chance against such men. As I watched them tearing the settlement apart in the search for us, I knew the time had come to leave. I grabbed two full water-skins, a loaf of hard, dry bread, and the leather pack containing my father's knife, my flint-and-steel, and some twine. Then I crept into the stony hills surrounding the settlement with my brother and sister in tow.

All I knew was that Father had gone to the north. We had heard of a village on the other side of the Stone Hills, but I had never been there and had no idea of how far away it was. We were all nearly dead of exhaustion and thirst when we finally found water on the fifth day...I had been carrying my sister for two days and nights. The wind had been our friend, stirring the dust to cover what tracks we left, but it chilled us to the bone at night.

We risked no fires, but huddled together for warmth, listening to the big-eared foxes gibbering and bark-howling in their harsh, eerie voices.

We continued north, eating grasshoppers and crickets and anything else we could find, until at last we saw the village in the distance. It had been there for quite some time, judging by the numerous stone dwellings and obvious, established marketplace. It existed largely because of a clear, bubbling spring that flowed from the stones—much larger than the one in our settlement—bringing life and prosperity. Trees stood here, too, but I wondered what was wrong with some of them. They looked as though they had lost most of their leaves, and some of the branches wilted and drooped like crippled, weary old men.

When we drew nearer, we saw the blackened bodies tethered to those trees—sad skeletons clad in scraps of charred flesh, lolling skulls open-mouthed as though still screaming. The worst were the remains of those who had been crucified—hung up alive and slowly tortured to death. I had never seen a man so savagely tormented before, but I have since learned what it means. Crucifixion was done only to the worst offenders. Why, then, had they crucified my father?

I knew him at once…what was left of him. Mercifully, my brother and sister did not see him at first. I had left them hidden, creeping closer to investigate, hoping I was wrong. He had been dead for several days, but his body still bore witness to the unspeakable pain he had endured. Another man, hanging nearby, was still alive, struggling to draw breath, his face a mask of agony, his face streaked with tears.

The people of that village had turned into madmen. Many had been scarred by the Sickness, and quite a number appeared to be still in the throes of it, judging by the blood on their faces. When the wind changed, I could smell the distant pile of bodies.

One of the scarred ones stood upon a wooden platform, yelling and waving his arms about in some sort of emphatic speech. His listeners were frightened—I could tell by the way they huddled together—but not nearly as frightened as I was of them. I did not yet fully realize the depth and breadth of savagery that fear can drive men to.

I heard Seth's cries as he was set upon—he had disobeyed, coming out of hiding to follow me unaware—but before I could leap to defend him, strong hands grabbed my arms.

"There's nothing you can do, boy," said a cold voice in a hissing whisper. "They have found him, and that has doomed him. The scarred ones will kill anyone of your race who is unmarked. You must come away with me now!"

I struggled, trying to cry out as a large hand clamped over my nose and mouth. I couldn't breathe, which gained my full attention for the moment.

"Stop struggling!" said the voice. "I am only one man, and you are only a scrawny little boy. If they find us, I will have to abandon you and your sister. I'd rather not do that."

To my horror, some men were dragging Seth down to the village, where they were soon joined by a ragged group of perhaps twenty other men and women. I could hear my brother crying.

The people screamed and bellowed in angry voices, chanting something in a tongue I did not know. Snarling and beating their breasts, they tied Seth to one of the charred trees amid the skeletons. He had stopped crying, now terrified into shocked silence, pale and helpless amid the twisted black tangle of bones. To my horror, he looked toward the hills, and his eyes met mine. I saw his lips move, speaking my name. Then his chest began heaving and he screamed in terror. He strained against his bonds…strained toward me, wailing, begging me to save him.

The stranger's grip tightened on me, though he allowed me to breathe again, knowing I would be too breathless to cry out. "They will be occupied with him for a while. We'll take advantage of that—you, your sister, and I." He took hold of my neck in one of his strong hands, clamping down until darkness took me, sparing me the spectacle of the terrible fate of my little brother, who had never done anything to harm anyone.

***

I awoke to the sound of wind hissing through the rocks, and the soft moaning of my little sister as she lay beside me, lost in a fitful dream. For a moment, I wondered whether I had been dreaming, too. I held that blessed hope for as long as I could, until the bruises on my neck spoke up and reminded me. *You're not dreaming. Father is dead, and Seth…he's gone, too.* I thought of the man who had taken Salina and me away from the village, my mind full of questions. *Who is he? Where has he gone? What does he want with us? What will he do to us?*

I tried to stay still, in case he was nearby. I didn't want him to know I was awake, but I couldn't see much of my surroundings, so at last I was forced to move my head. I heard a rustling noise from behind me as the man, who was wrapped in a ripped, dusty bedroll, came to life.

"Are we awake?" he asked, his bright eyes peering intelligently from a very dirty, brown-bearded face.

I did not reply, but turned back to my little sister, who was still dreaming. Her small, damp body shook with terror until her eyes snapped open and she cried out, jerking into wakefulness and pushing away from me with both hands.

I let her alone, knowing she would realize she had been dreaming. When she did, she started to cry and I took her into my arms.

"Sounds like we're all awake now," drawled the bearded man, whose name, I learned, was Caspar. "We'd better get moving. We need to find water today or tomorrow at the latest."

I knew better than to argue, following along behind him, holding my sister's hand. She was hungry, and said so.

"Here you are, little one. Better make it last," said Caspar, tossing her a strip of some kind of dried mix of meat and fruit. Salina, who was quite thoughtful for a girl of five, broke the strip in two and handed half to me. Then she took one small bite and put the rest in her pocket. We did find water the next morning, and again the next, as we traveled farther north. We said very little to one another until the fourth day, when I finally summoned the courage to ask about my brother, Seth.

"Did they do what I think they did?" I asked.

Caspar rubbed his weary eyes with grubby fingers. "You know they did. They burned him alive."

"But *why*? And why did they kill my father? He only went there to help…and to seek help."

"Because he was unmarked."

"What does *that* mean?" I asked, confused and getting angrier by the minute.

"It means you, your father, and your brother and sister have come from a place of pestilence, yet you remain unmarked. In their minds, you are evil beings who bring the Sickness among men and remain untouched by it. Those people are survivors—you saw the scars on their faces—and they believe that only by killing you can they keep the Sickness at bay."

"But we didn't bring any sickness. It came in a merchant caravan," I said, my cheeks hot with indignation.

"I know," said Caspar. "But the Sickness has made them mad. They cannot care for themselves any more. They won't live long…they're sure to starve before the year is out. And they've witnessed horrible things happening to ones they loved—things which they are convinced came from people like you. There's no point in trying to make sense of it, believe me."

That night, I curled up with Salina in Caspar's spare bedroll until she fell asleep. Then I rose and went out under the moon. I wanted to scream at it. I wanted to rage against whoever was responsible for the repulsive idea that my father, or six-year-old Seth, who barely knew how to tie his own boot-laces, could ever be blamed for such a horrible thing as the Sickness. That they could ever be thought of as "evil beings."

He says they will all be dead soon? Good. It's no less than they deserve. Mother was like them—she bore the scars, but she never blamed anyone. She never hurt anyone.

By the time morning came, I hated them all.

We had traveled with Caspar for nearly a fortnight when he started to change. He moved slower, tired more quickly, and grew irritable.

"Are you all right?" I asked him one night. "You're not sick, are you?"

"Of course not!" he snapped. "I've been through hell already and the Sickness hasn't gotten me. Now don't mention it again!"

His voice may have been steady, but I could see the fear in his eyes, and I felt a strong desire to keep Salina away from him from then on.

The nights had gotten colder the farther north we traveled; Caspar had led us toward some tall hills covered with sparsely-scattered trees, hoping for shelter from the wind.

"I don't like sleeping in his blankets," whispered Salina. "They're full of fleas!"

"Well, they're all we've got," I whispered back, fighting the urge to start scratching the itches that had suddenly appeared at the very mention of fleas. But they were real enough. I saw the red marks they made on me, on my sister, and on Caspar. He had caught a ground-squirrel in a snare several nights before. Perhaps that was where they had come from.

When we awoke the next morning, we knew something was wrong. Caspar was coughing, his eyes red-rimmed and fevered. I could feel the heat rolling off of him. He pulled the canvas over his head and moaned. "Oh, Lord of Heaven…after all this time…please, not this!"

My sister pulled back into her own tangle of blankets, knowing enough to be afraid of him. "Stay here," I told her. "Maybe he just needs some water."

I offered him one of our water-skins, hoping I would not smell the Sickness on him, but it was rampaging through him like a grass fire in a high wind. The sores were already erupting on his cheeks and forehead. The rag into which he had been coughing was soaked with blood. I left him the water-skin, and I had not the slightest idea of where he had been leading us or why, but I would not remain to see if he would die or go mad. I had failed Seth, but I could still protect Salina. Nothing else mattered.

Caspar must have realized we were leaving him. I heard his voice, cracked and full of pain, drifting from the bedroll. "Please don't leave me…I need you. Please help me…"

I took the other water-skin, the spare bedroll, and a few strips of dried meat from his pack. Salina was reluctant to leave him, for her heart was still open to pity and mercy, but I gave her no choice. "Thank you for saving us," I muttered. "May the Lord of Heaven reward you." Then I turned from him and never looked back.

***

We kept to our northward course, guided by the stars. At times I wondered about the wisdom of it, as the nights were cold enough already and the path we took seemed to get steeper and more arduous as the days passed. We ran out of food on the second day after we left Caspar. After that we ate whatever we could catch, which wasn't much. We even ate the little, hopping fleas from the bedroll, an act which brought Salina quite a bit of satisfaction. "Bite *me*, will you? Let's see how you like being bitten." She crushed their flat little bodies carefully between strong front teeth.

All right—we didn't exactly eat them. But they are hard to kill, and biting them is a sure way to do it. I'm sure we swallowed some, intentionally or not.

One cannot survive long on a diet of fleas, and grasshoppers were becoming increasingly hard to find. I have eaten many of them out of necessity over the course of my life—fried, dipped in honey, powdered with hot spices—and I have always considered them disgusting no matter what they are flavored with. Back then, lost and desperate, we would have paid a fortune in king's gold for them. These days, I prefer to avoid eating any creature with more than four legs.

Salina was a strong little girl, but the cold and lack of food had weakened her. When she first had the dream about the Moon Man, I thought she was fevered. She woke up shaking with terror, clutching my arm. I felt her forehead…she wasn't fevered. "Salina, it's all right. Just a bad dream."

"No…no it's not. The Moon Man is coming," she said in a voice I hadn't heard since she was about two and a half.

"What 'Moon Man?' Who's that?" I muttered, knowing it was just some nonsense conceived in her five-year-old mind.

"Don't ask me to talk about him now. He might hear us," she whispered. "He's real. The Moon Man is *real.*"

Every night thereafter, Salina spoke of the Moon Man. She was afraid to go to sleep because of him, but she wouldn't travel under the moon, either. She sat, wide-eyed and fearful, with the bedroll drawn up to her chin. At last, overcome by weariness, she would sag over into sleep. If she was lucky, she wouldn't dream.

If she was unlucky, she would wake screaming. "Soon the moon will be big and yellow…that's when he'll come to get us!" she cried. "We have to get to a house—we have to have people to protect us. Lots of people! *Big* people!"

"Well, we can't," I grumbled. "There aren't any houses around here, and in case you haven't noticed, the only big people we've seen have been horrible. Even Caspar would have ended up horrible. So just stop thinking about it!"

She began to whimper, digging her knuckles into her eyes, which were swollen from crying, making me feel like the most terrible, meanest person in the world. I patted her shoulder. "Listen, Salina, we have father's axe. If this Moon Man comes, I won't let him get you. I promise, all right?"

She stopped crying and looked up at me, round-eyed. Then she said something that should never have come from the mouth of anyone so young. "You don't understand. He *eats* people, Glennroy. The Moon Man comes out under the yellow moon...and he *eats people!* He'll use father's axe to chop us up. Don't you think he won't." She folded her arms in front of her. "We have to find a house."

I could see there was no reasoning with her. "All right. We'll look for a house." At least it would keep her moving.

Before the incident with the Moon Man, I had not known of my sister's gift. But when the moon rose over the horizon a few days later, an enormous golden orb tinged with rusty orange, I heard the horrible cries for the first time. They sounded like someone howling in unspeakable pain.

"It's the Moon Man," whispered Salina. "He's coming tonight!"

The horrible cry came again. It sounded closer than the last. "We'd better find a good hiding place," I said, hoping not to be condemned to eternal torment for committing the sin of not listening to my sister.

"It won't matter too much," said Salina. "He can smell us, anyway."

"*Now* you tell me. Come on."

We found the best hiding place we could, crouching amid the dark shadows cast by a tumble of stones. The Moon Man had gone strangely quiet, for which I was both grateful and afraid. Was he quiet because he was going away, or because he was on the hunt?

When the horrible howling came again, he was close enough that we could see him. He stood tall on a rock, silhouetted against the now pale gold moon, his head thrown back like a wolf's. He was painfully thin and covered with scars—the mark of his madness—his hair a matted tangle full of dead grass and thorns. Around his neck was a necklace of bones, and he carried a large thigh-bone in one gnarled, ragged-nailed hand.

Today, as a man, I cannot be certain that bone was human. As an eleven-year-old boy, I was absolutely certain. *He eats people, Glennroy…*

When the Moon Man's head snapped around, and his eyes fixed on our pile of stones, I knew what I had to do. I waited…waited until he drew near enough. He was obviously starving—so were we all—but his desperate hope of finding prey made him careless. He didn't know who or what was crouched in that pile of stones. *Come on, you filthy creature—come and get me. That's it…come on! A little closer, please.* I looked over at Salina and raised father's axe just enough for her to see. She nodded. I saw her draw a couple of deep, resolute breaths. Then she leaped up and uttered the loudest, most piercing scream she could manage, throwing both hands in the air.

The Moon Man jumped back, cringing and shaking his head. She had startled him—but only for a moment. It was all I needed. I leaped up and rushed toward him, the hand-axe glinting in the golden light, and I buried it in the side of the Moon Man's neck. He wasn't nearly as large a man as he had appeared, and he fell to one knee, cawing like a wounded crow and clawing at the gushing wound on his neck. I knew it would kill him—no one bleeds like that and lives for very long—but I screamed and struck again, this time at the back of his neck, where the spine was. He dropped in a heap of filthy limbs and matted hair.

That was it. I had killed my first man.

I remember being surprised at how easy it was. I had been prepared for a struggle, to die for my sister if need be, yet two well-placed blows was all it took. That and a startled man armed with a thigh bone against a fiercely motivated boy wielding sharpened steel.

Salina was crying now, and she ran to me for comfort.

"You killed him! You killed the Moon Man!"

"I promised I would protect you, remember?" Without warning, the strength drained out of me, and I fell over onto the stony ground.

"No, Glennroy...we have to move away from here," said Salina, tugging on my arm. "You can't sleep yet. We shouldn't stay near the Moon Man, even if he's dead."

My head was swimming and the stars wavered in and out of focus in a very unpleasant manner, but I took her point, crawling after her until my senses returned and the night air revived me a little. When Salina thought we were finally far enough away from what remained of the Moon Man, she let me fall into an exhausted sleep.

In the morning she brought me a clutch of bird's eggs she had found—a real gift, our first blessing in a long time. We shared them equally, but she gave one back at the last. "You're bigger, and you worked hard last night."

"So did you," I said, smiling at her. "It takes a lot to scream that loud!" I did, however, take the egg. I don't care for raw eggs—as a man, I won't eat them unless desperate. But back then they were ambrosial. I sucked out every bit, then ate the shells for good measure.

When we had finished, we rested again. Salina kept watching me with solemn eyes, and I wondered what she was thinking.

"Glennroy...when you killed the Moon Man, did you like it?"

"What do you mean? I killed him because I had to!"

"But...did you *like* it?"

I thought for a moment. Why would she ask such a question? And how should I answer it? I thought some more. As I was killing that mad, subhuman creature—a creature bent on destroying my sister and me—I had imagined I was killing every single one of the monsters who had murdered my father and my brother. I imagined I was burying father's axe in every one of their filthy necks, and it should have felt good. It should have, but I felt nothing. The Moon Man might as well have been a flea between my front teeth. I felt nothing at all.

"Father says we're not supposed to kill people," I said at last. "We should only kill if we have to."

That seemed to satisfy her at the time, but she said one last thing before she fell asleep. "You'll kill a lot of people someday, Glennroy. You would never kill me, would you?"

I swallowed, feeling a chill take hold of me. "What sort of stupid question is *that?*" I said, trying to sound annoyed rather than alarmed. "Now, go to sleep."

She smiled at me, turned over onto her other side, and closed her eyes.

***

Before we moved on, I went back to where we had left the Moon Man's body. To my surprise, there was no trace of it, other than the marks in the dust where something large and heavy had dragged it away. I shuddered, taking notice of the enormous footprints all around the area. I had no idea what had made them, but the claw-marks at the end of each of the four toes made me shudder. *It's a good thing we moved as far away as we did. Whatever this thing was, we're lucky it was satisfied with only one carcass last night.* From that day, I viewed my little sister with an entirely new level of respect.

We saw the smoke from a distant campfire after two days with almost no water and very little to eat. There was more green here, but the leathery shrubs were still dry and we had seen no sign of rain. At least there was shade.

Salina didn't have enough strength to walk anymore. I had been carrying her since breakfast, which had consisted of a handful of shiny black beetles and some soft, white grubs I had found underneath a rock. We needed to be careful, as some crawly-things could make you very sick if you ate them, and we didn't know many of the ones found in the lands we traveled through. These black ones, thankfully, could be eaten safely.

Though I was afraid of whoever had made the fire, I knew we had no choice but to make for it. Salina, at least, would die for certain if she didn't get some good food and a warm place to sleep. I wondered how far away the smoke was—it didn't look that bad, but I knew that things weren't always as they appeared. Sometimes you can think a line of smoke is just over the next rise, but that might be miles away. I couldn't worry about that at the time, so I just kept putting one foot in front of the other.

Then came the moment when I could no longer put any of my feet anywhere. I had come up against an obstacle that I could not get over, and I hadn't the strength to go around it. I sank down onto the ground, making sure that Salina and I were well away from the edge of the deep gorge blocking our path, and tried not to weep. *Maybe I should just throw us both in,* I thought. *Salina's barely alive as it is. At least it would be quick...probably.*

I remembered one of our goats who had, against all the usual tendencies of his race, fallen from a pinnacle of stone in an attempt to grab a bite of thorn-bush. The goat's end hadn't been quick at all, as we couldn't get to it to ease its suffering. No...throwing ourselves into the gorge wouldn't serve at all.

My legs cramped from lack of water and salt, I was almost too weary to draw breath, I had stopped shivering in the cold some time ago, and I was beginning to see

The Shadow-Man

things that weren't there. I closed my eyes, hugged Salina, and gave myself over to darkness.

***

When I came to, I could hear the blessed sound of water running. I could smell it, too…river water, if I knew anything at all. We were at the bottom of the gorge.

As soon as my eyes could focus, I saw the grey-and-rust-banded cliffs towering on either side. *Salina…where is my sister?* I looked around for her, reaching as far as I could, as I was too weak to get up. "Salina? Salina!"

A pair of booted legs appeared beside my head, and a man knelt down, placing a hand on my shoulder. "The little girl is here. She's picking up some, though we all thought she would die. She's stronger than she looks—just like you. You must be her brother, right?"

I nodded.

"What's your name, Big Brother?"

"Glennroy, son of Glenndon."

"Well, Glennroy, you'll get a new name here. Everyone does. You'll be getting a new start in life now that you're with us. It would seem to me that you and your sister have escaped from your own village, and we're wondering whether the Sickness has been there. I'm thinking you and your sister didn't get sick, but those who did are trying to kill you now. Am I right?"

I nodded.

"Are any others left alive and unmarked?"

"I don't know…I don't know of any," I said, my head beginning to swim again.

"That's fine. Now sleep, and I'll see what I can do about finding you something good to eat when you wake up. Drink this in the meantime—it's very sustaining."

He held a vessel to my lips, and I drank. It was warm, fruity, and wonderful. I slept well for the first time in weeks.

When I awoke, I took stock of my situation. Apparently there were a number of people here. I heard many voices, both male and female. They had dressed me in clean clothes, no doubt burning the rags I had been wearing—I know I would have. But when I lifted my new tunic and looked beneath it, I saw a boy who was barely alive. My bones were barely covered by anything except skin, which was mottled with bruises and flea-bites. *What a mess,* I thought, a wave of light-headedness coming over me. *I can't even stand to look at myself.*

As if on cue, I heard the same man's voice again. He startled me, having approached from behind. "Your sister is in better shape than you are, don't worry," he said. "And you can relax. No one will hurt you here. You've come to a very lucky place—perhaps the only one where you'll be welcome. You must now put all that has happened in your life—everyone you have known—behind you. We will be your family now, if you will accept us."

He handed me a bowl of warm goat's milk sweetened with wild honey. "Only drink this if you are willing," he said. "Otherwise, you are free to leave. Your sister, however, has elected to stay."

Of course she has, I thought. *What choice did she have? What choice do I have, in fact?*

I sat up and looked around. I could see other children running and chasing one another. I heard them laughing. It didn't seem to be a bad place, and I knew I could never leave Salina, anyway. I took the bowl, and I drank.

***

The Shadow-Man

The man's name was Thurston, and he looked like a northerner. I know that now, though I had rarely laid eyes on any when I was a boy. There were several northern children in the group, though, as well as almond-eyed easterners, though most were brown-skinned sutherlings like Salina and me. Thurston explained that he and the others called themselves "Gleaners." It was their job to find and rescue any and all children who had been orphaned by the Sickness. Some of the rescued children had obviously gotten sick and recovered, as evidenced by the scarring on their bodies. When I saw them I shrank back, remembering the Moon Man.

"Don't worry," said Thurston. "They're not mad—at least not in the way you're thinking. They have been damaged, and their heads are a little...muddled. You'll find they do some odd things, but they won't hurt you. They don't have an adult's capacity to fear and blame others. Would you like to see your sister now?"

I was still too weak to walk, so Thurston brought Salina to me, along with an older woman. Salina didn't fling herself into my waiting arms, as I had expected her to. She sat quietly down beside me, her eyes round and solemn. "I thought you had died," she said at last. "I was so afraid...I didn't want to leave you, and I didn't know what to do."

"She's the one who led us to you," said Thurston. "She thought you were dead, and she used the last of her strength to build a fire—it was the smoke that drew our attention."

"You...built a *fire?*" I stammered, trying to imagine her struggles with the flint-and-steel.

"I know. You told me not to touch your things, but I couldn't think of anything else to do," she said, obviously on the edge of tears.

I turned to Thurston. "I was afraid to do that, lest it

draw the attention of...you know, unfriendly folk. I didn't know whether you would help us or burn us alive."

"Well, I guess Salina knew you had nothing to lose," said Thurston.

"And now someone's feeling guilty—perhaps you should reassure her," said the older woman, putting a comforting hand on Salina's shoulder.

"Hulda looks after me," said Salina, and then burst into tears. I took her in my arms and held her for several minutes, telling her over and over that she had done the right thing, that I was proud of her. But there was something down inside me that didn't believe, and she could feel it. We were alive, and these people appeared to be taking good care of us, but I didn't trust them.

"Please, Glennroy," she whispered. "Please...try to be happy. I want you to be happy."

I wanted to tell her that no one who has ever seen what I had seen—his father crucified for absolutely no reason at all, his harmless little brother burned alive, a madman who eats people and howls like a beast—could ever be happy. I wanted to warn her that happiness is a thing few people ever attain. I had known that even then, and I am doubly convinced of it now. But all I could do was try to reassure her, and she seemed to accept it, though I thought I saw a trace of doubt in her eyes.

***

We had a long journey ahead of us. I learned from the other children that the Gleaners had been gathering them—marked or unmarked—for several months. They had come from the southeast, moved northward and then westward, but now had turned south again. They were returning home.

"Home? Where's that?" I asked.

"Somewhere over the inland sea," said a boy named Asher, who was about my age. I had decided to like him when he shared a pouch of dried figs with Salina and me.

"What inland sea? I've never heard of such a thing," I said.

"Well, neither had I. And my home was farther north than yours. The inland sea is south," said Asher.

I had been given a new name—they called me Beltran, which means raven in some tongue or other. Apparently ravens had gathered, preparing to feast on what was left of me, when I was found. My hair is raven-black as well. I guess it was as good a name as any. My sister had been re-named Silva, meaning "inner eye." Had someone else become aware of her abilities?

We were expected to work, and work hard. The bravest of the boys were sent into the remains of villages ravaged by the Sickness, instructed to steal whatever food and valuables they could find. Usually the settlements were deserted, but one could never be sure. We lost one of the boys to a madman, who had apparently killed all the other surviving members of his clan. He leaped out from behind a row of water-barrels, grabbed the unfortunate boy by the hair, and cut his throat, nearly taking his head off. The boy didn't even have the chance to scream. We shot the madman down like the dog he had become.

Asher and I volunteered to replace the dead boy, and we soon discovered we made a pretty good team. I was graceful and stealthy—Asher was smart. He seemed to know where things of value could be found, and we never returned empty-handed. He was shy, though, especially about taking his clothes off. It got warmer and more humid as we continued southward, so I stripped down to a sleeveless tunic and breechclout, but Asher kept his full breeches and long sleeves. Finally, one very warm and sultry night, I convinced him. Then I saw why they had named him Asher.

Both legs and his left forearm were covered with terrible scars, only recently formed. Only one thing makes scars like that, and I knew that Asher had been tied to a tree and set aflame. The Gleaners had rescued him before he could burn to death, killing his tormentors, but he had suffered terrible disfigurement. That he was still alive was a testimony to his inherent toughness. I admired his spirit. He had kept some of his good humor in spite of everything. In fact, Asher loved a good prank and would often arrange one at someone else's expense. He soon enlisted my aid and, though I have little use for such things, I went along. I wondered what demons tormented him at night—whether laughter made them go back into the dark for a while.

I rarely saw my sister, except at night, when she insisted on sleeping beside me. They worked her fairly hard, too—she and the other little girls learned the skills they would need in order to take care of men. Silva stitched my tunic when it came apart, showing me the small, neat stitches with pride. She learned to cook, after a fashion, as she had no aptitude for it. She received many a withering look from the other girls, and it hurt her feelings.

One night, as she lay beside me, I could hear her crying.

"What is it, Salina?" We always called one another by our real names, though it was forbidden. She stopped crying and turned her back to me.

"I can't tell you."

"You can tell me anything. You know that—I'm your brother," I said. "Now, what's wrong? Why are you crying?"

"I'm not crying," she said with a sniffle.

The Shadow-Man

"Oh, sorry, my mistake. Now what's wrong?"

"I can't tell you. I won't," she said, her voice flat and emotionless. "I won't, and you can't make me."

"Is it the dreams again? Have you seen something you don't like?" I asked, though I had already told myself I really didn't want to know. I was afraid of Salina's dreams—rightly so.

"I...I don't know," she said, which meant that she really *did* know. She just didn't want to say. *Best just leave it alone,* I thought. *She'll tell you when she's ready.* But then, she spoke again.

"Stay out of the dark, Glennroy. Stay out of the dark, or you'll be there forever. I can't go there with you." She threw off her blanket, got to her feet, and moved to sit beside the dying embers of a nearby cook-fire, huddling over the red-gold light as though the darkness around me was already too deep for her liking.

***

We came to our destination at last—the inland sea. I had never seen such a vast expanse of water before, and it filled me with a sort of terrified awe, quite understandable since I didn't yet know how to swim. "What do we do now?" I asked Asher. "Follow it around? Where is the City they have been speaking of?

"Oh, we won't be going around," said a young man named Ulrich. "That would take far too long. We'll be crossing it."

"How?" I asked, incredulous. "There are no boats!"

"They're called ships, dunderhead. They'll be lighting the signal fires any minute now."

"What signal fires?"

Ulrich sighed, stroking the beginnings of his scruffy

beard with a loving hand. "The ones that tell the King's men we've come back. Just be quiet, watch, and learn!"

This was my first experience with signal-fires, though the technique had been around for a thousand years at least. When a message needed to be carried over great distance, huge piles of wood and pitch would be built along the way. These were manned by watchmen, whose only task was to set them aflame at the right time. They had been placed in such a way that they could easily be seen by the next watcher in line—usually on a mountain or hilltop.

I saw the first one go up, sending a column of black smoke high into the air. "Look, there!" said Ulrich, pointing to the east. A second column had appeared almost as quickly as the first. Then I saw a third one in the distance. It won't take long to get the message back, and then they'll send the ships," said Ulrich with a smile. "It will take a while for them to get here, of course, but we have arrived at the right time.

"What's this place like…the one where we're going?" I asked him.

"Like nothing you've ever seen before," said Ulrich. "Assuming, of course, that it's still the same as I left it three years ago."

I must tell you that I have never liked traveling on a ship—I hated it when I was a boy, and I hate it now. I might have been fine had I been sailing alone, but I don't like the smell, I don't like the lack of freedom, and I detest being crowded in with a lot of other people, some of whom seemed to have a strange aversion to cleanliness.

Fortunately, I have never been afraid of heights, as we had to scale cliffs and climb tall rocks to get to our sheep and goats sometimes. As such, I spent much of my time perched on the single mast, reveling in the feel of the

The Shadow-Man

wind. I was lucky—poor Asher spent much of his time heaving into a bucket.

I didn't see my sister at all—the women and girls were kept separate throughout the voyage, lest the sailors be tempted to misbehave. Usually occupied with their tasks aboard ship, the men didn't seem unhappy or oppressed, which I took as a good sign. I asked them how long it would take to arrive at the place they called Orovar, the Golden Shore.

"Ask the Wind. She makes the time pass, or not pass," they said. "You'll know when you see it." They had, by this time, stopped scolding me for climbing the mast. If I insisted on being up there, I could at least keep a lookout.

When we finally arrived, I understood what they had meant by "you'll know when you see it." You couldn't see the City at first, though the smoke told you it was there. It lay behind tall sea-cliffs of bright golden stone banded with warm pink and creamy white. The sun hit them just right, and I gasped in awe at their beauty, made especially vibrant by the contrast with the deep blue-green water that crashed against them in a flurry of white and pale-green foam. I called down to the sailors, who, naturally, were not surprised by my revelation. "Come down, little raven. The tide is rising, and things might get a little rough until we find the harbor—wouldn't want you to learn to fly now!"

I understood what they meant as the ship was tossed about by the currents running into one another—one deep and cold, the other warm. We caught this one, riding it straight toward the cliffs on the rising tide. It carried us through a narrow opening which broadened out into a calm harbor. Then I saw the City.

I have since visited a few of the great realms, and, compared with them, Orovar was small and unimpressive, but it certainly impressed me as a boy. We had all crowded up on deck for a look—even Asher, though his pale face was still greenish. The City held all the promise a boy of my age could ask for. I hoped I would find adventure, excitement, maybe even prosperity here. And I could hardly wait to get off the crowded deck of the ship.

I looked around for my sister, but did not see her. *She'll be all right. They've been taking good care of her,* I told myself. I thought I was far too involved in my own concerns to worry about it, but something nagged at me anyway. *Remember your promise to her. Don't trust them. Remember your promise…*

My sister, as it happened, was still down in the hold, huddled in a corner and weeping. Unable to coax her out, they had to carry her off the ship, though she cried and begged them not to. It seemed she had already been treated to some insight as to what awaited her on the Golden Shore.

***

I flattered my way into a friendship with Ulrich, and I had learned quite a lot from him concerning Orovar. In the beginning it was merely a stop on the main southern trade route. Its people had been mostly of sutherling descent, but soon mingled with folk of other races when sailors or tradesmen would decide it was time to give up the wandering life. Several smaller communities had bloomed outside its boundaries, often founded by members of trade guilds. Resources and raw materials came either directly from the land and sea or in the form of ships laden with goods.

A King and his ministers ruled the City, which had enjoyed an orderly and peaceful, if unexciting, past. Then came the Sickness, changing everything as it always did.

The Shadow-Man

Orovar had been one of the first to feel the darkness of death—nearly seven years had come and gone since the first sailor spouted blood on the deck. She had lost five of every seven people, including many of the King's ministers. The King himself was spared, but he became reclusive, locking the City down and imposing very strict laws on her citizens. Ulrich admitted that he had never seen King Darius. "He is said to be wise, but unforgiving."

Thurston, of course, had come along on the voyage. He took it upon himself to instruct us as we prepared to disembark. "You must not question any decree or order that comes from the King or his ministers. To do so would bring severe penalty. No one will care how young or foolish you are—all are bound by the same laws here."

"Sounds like a wonderfully friendly place," muttered Asher.

"Indeed," I said. "We haven't even arrived, and they're already warning us about severe penalties. But Ulrich says Orovar needs people to replenish itself, which is why we have been brought here. Surely, after taking all the trouble to find and retrieve us, they won't be imposing severe penalties just yet. That's what the Gleaners are for… to collect any and all survivors of the Sickness. Ulrich says unmarked children who have lost their families are especially prized—that's you and me."

I shivered as I walked down the gang-plank into my new home, though the weather was fine and warm. It didn't take me long to realize how cold it was in Orovar. People seemed happy and prosperous on the surface, but there was a chill—a detachment—that seemed to pervade every aspect of their lives. My sister would have felt it right away, and it would have terrified her. Later I realized the source of the chill—the City cared only for itself. We were being made welcome, but I sensed I would only be as welcome or valued as the service I could provide. One oddity: I saw no beggars in the streets, and I wondered why.

At the time, I only knew that I wouldn't have to worry about the Sickness, being hunted by madmen, or starving to death. If you have never experienced starvation, you cannot understand how important food is to someone who has. When they herded us into the holding facility, I didn't care one bit for the loss of personal freedom. I shook off my misgivings, willingly gave up my few possessions, and didn't care that I was dressed in the same drab attire as everyone else. All I cared about was being fed three times a day, as they had promised. I also learned that being well fed required absolute obedience and cooperation.

I was herded into a holding yard with many other children, including Salina, who would not leave my side. She would not speak to anyone, either, except at night. Then she would huddle in my arms and whisper.

"Cold…the people are cold. The place is bad, Glennroy. It's bad. We should leave."

"Well, we can't leave," I said. "I do wish you'd stop saying such things. They're going to think you've gone mad. Besides, it's not so bad…at least they feed us."

If you followed all the rules, you were fed. If you got along with the others, you were fed. But if you shared your food with anyone else, you would find your next ration cut drastically. I tried to share with Salina, who always received less than I did. When they discovered this, I was told that I was receiving more food than I needed if I would give it away. The ration I received that day was less than half of what I was used to, and I shared no more with anyone.

I have since realized that we were being observed the

entire time we were in the holding-yard. Every now and then a man would appear and call out someone's name. That person would then leave the yard, never to return. Word had spread that you would be called out when the City had a use for you—that this was a good thing.

They called Salina in the first week, no doubt having found a use for her already. I wondered what they had in mind for her. She cried when they led her away, and I couldn't comfort her. I had been too far away, and didn't get to her in time.

They called Asher a week later. "Don't worry, Beltran. They'll call you next," he said, clasping my hand. Then he was gone, and I had no one to be concerned for except myself. I could hardly wait until they called my name.

There were both unmarked and scarred survivors in the yard. I had learned that the scarred ones were either dull-witted, unpredictable, or downright mean, and I avoided them whenever I could. A gang of six bigger boys delighted in intimidating the rest of us, stealing our food and promising retaliation if we reported them. They could hurt you so that no one would see, and would threaten anyone who got in their way. One day, they strode up to me and snatched my food away before I could blink.

I had been eating reasonably well for several weeks, and so I didn't react with quite as much fury as I might have. Instead I carefully unlaced the leather cord from the front of my tunic, waited until they thought I had accepted my fate, crept up behind one of them, and slipped the cord around his neck.

"If you move, I'll kill you," I whispered. "You won't even make a sound. Now, if you would like to remain alive, nod once."

He did.

"Very well. You and your friends will leave me alone in

the future. You will not take my food, understand?"

Another nod.

"Good. And remember...once we are out of this place, I'll treat you the same way. If I see you, you'll leave me alone. Otherwise, you'll disappear. I know how to do that, too."

Of course, I was bluffing. I had no idea of how to make anyone disappear, though I certainly have one now. But I know to this day that I could have killed him had he tried to thwart me. That's what got my name called the next day.

***

They took me away with no fanfare at all—they didn't even speak to me. I soon found myself in a stark, grey cell with stone walls, a straw mattress on the floor, a vessel of water, a basin for washing in, and a chamber-pot. *What, am I in prison now? No...not a prison. From what I've heard of them, this window would be too big, and there are no bars on it. Besides...it's way too clean here.* The window was too high to see anything but sky, so I jumped, grabbed the stone sill, and tried to haul myself up for a look. I could hear what sounded like marching feet and the clash of wood and steel, but I had grown weaker in confinement and my arms gave out. I dropped down to the well-swept floor, just in time for the heavy wooden door to swing open.

A man loomed in the doorway, so large he almost filled it entirely. "Beltran, is it?" he said.

I tried to sound confident. "Yes sir. Beltran."

"You have been accepted into the ranks of the hopeful—those who would defend the City. As a new recruit, your duty is to do what you're told, when you're told. You will not question orders or instructions, ever. If you prove worthy, you will be trained. If not, you will find employment in a much less prestigious vocation. Understand?"

I nodded.

"Good. We have been watching you. It would be a shame to see you mucking out pig-pens for the rest of your life, wouldn't it?"

I nodded again.

"Can you read? No? Well, that's a pity, but we'll soon remedy it. You'll just have to remember. You'll hear a bell every morning, and someone will come to get you. You should be out of bed and fully dressed when they come." He drew forth a paper-wrapped parcel from a satchel and handed it to me. "Put these on. Tonight you will be fed in your room, but starting tomorrow you'll eat with the others. Get some sleep. You'll have a full day of training ahead of you."

He turned and swung the door shut before I could even ask his name.

***

My father had always taught me to think for myself, but he also taught me the value of keeping my head down. I knew better than to be defiant or stubborn, at least in the beginning. I settled into my training, having learned that the people who now had control of my life held the same indifference to human frailties as the rest of the citizens did. This is what happens when you throw people together who have almost nothing in common other than grief and loss. We had all withdrawn into little islands, isolating ourselves from pain. If we didn't get to know our neighbors, we didn't have to care about what happened to them.

The only person I had really befriended since my rescue was Asher, and I had not seen him since they called his name in the holding-yard. I wondered where they had taken him, hoping that maybe he would be training with me, but I would soon be disappointed. Asher and I were friends, but we were very different people. He was a lot smarter than I was. At the time, I imagined he had been selected for something other than bashing and hacking at people.

Orovar was rapidly regaining its former glory, if one could call it that. The King had ordered the gathering and assembly of survivors—after all, what is a King without subjects? And the primary goal seemed to be training the City's military, which seemed odd to me at first. I had assumed that the people capable of organizing any sort of attack were dead, and the survivors had been brought here and sworn in as Citizens already. Eventually I would realize what the King was really afraid of.

I was sworn in as a Citizen on the first morning of training. I remember the oath well—I had to repeat it under every full moon for the next ten years. I swore to defend the King at all costs, to devote my mind and body to the betterment of Orovar, to always obey the orders of my superiors, and to never organize or participate in any act of rebellion, on pain of death. Later, I would swear a different sort of oath.

My schedule was highly regimented and controlled—eating, sleeping, training, studying. I learned to read and write, though I had no love for it at the time, and to fight with various weapons as well as hand-to-hand.

Regrettably, I had made an enemy in the holding-yard—the boy I had threatened to strangle. His name was Jamar, and I suppose I can't blame him for hating me. He had joined in with a gang of larger, more aggressive young men, several of whom bore the scars of Sickness. I knew how dangerous they were, and I tried to avoid them.

Except for my own sister, I held little regard for people. What they had done to my father and little brother had taught me that. I have no doubt that some had even turned on their own relations. Stupid, fearful people...they didn't matter to me. They could be used and then abandoned—I certainly didn't need to care about them or their fates. I had realized something else, too...that I was afraid of them. Of what they would do. The only way to quell those fears was to become powerful and fearsome myself. Then they would leave me alone.

This attitude made me quite a force in the training-yard, at least among eleven and twelve-year-olds. I swung my ironwood practice weapons—weighted exactly the same as their steel counterparts—with fervor. Accuracy and precision came later. I imagined my opponents were among the terrible mob that had tortured and killed my brother. Soon no one in my training group wanted to spar with me. I had no friends, and I didn't care.

When I went to lessons, I asked about my sister. They told me she was doing well, but that I would not be allowed to visit her until I had completed my training. "Your sister is in training, too," they said. "She is learning what she needs to learn, as you must." Then it was all reading, writing, and numbers...the only area where I could excel.

When I suffered my first real humiliation, it was outside the training arena. I had received a message from my Captain asking that I meet him in the courtyard behind the kitchens, where the rubbish was held until it could be hauled away. I had thought it strange, but I had sworn never to disobey an order.

At first, I saw no one waiting there. When Jamar and

his cronies, three of whom had at least five years and forty pounds on me, emerged from the shadows, I knew I was unlikely to leave unscathed. They carried no weapons—raising a real weapon against a fellow cadet carried the most severe punishment—but their hands looked quite lethal enough for me. Jamar held a loose length of cord in one hand. "I believe you might have lost this," he said, his eyes full of hate. "I'll just give it back to you, now, shall I?"

I panicked, looking around for any escape, outnumbered five to one. I had to better the odds, or I was dead.

"A shame you can't face me alone, Jamar," I said. "You're no match for me on your own, so I shouldn't be surprised that you bring along four bigger, stronger, better fighters to aid you. You're the biggest coward in the world!"

This appeal to his pride failed, as he had none. He and his gang leaped forward, intending to grab me.

How I managed to evade them I don't know, but I wrenched my arm so badly that I couldn't hold my sword up for nearly a month. I ended up in the only place I knew they wouldn't follow—the compost pit. At the time, the prevailing substance was fish heads. We ate a lot of fish in Orovar.

They laughed and left me to wallow, gasping and retching, as Jamar threw the cord at me. I later put it to good use, and I have it still. I learned a few things on that day. One was never to go against my own inner senses—if something didn't seem right, I wouldn't do it. The other was that stink washes off.

Unfortunately, this one didn't wash off quite soon enough, and I soon acquired the nickname "Fish-bait," which stuck with me until I left the training academy. But

The Shadow-Man

the harder I trained, the more I practiced, the more formidable I became. Soon the name "Fish-bait" was spoken with respect. I could live with that.

It wasn't an easy life. I asked after my sister each day at lessons, was told that she was well and that I could not see her until I had finished my training. Every day, the same question and answer. I did it because I loathed my language teacher and I thought it would annoy him, but also because I believed that as long as I asked each day, Salina would be all right. I didn't know where she was, or what they were doing to her. I saw plenty of young girls while I was abroad in the City, but never caught even a glimpse of her.

I was barely sixteen years old when I finally passed my first test, earning my acceptance into the lower ranks of the city guard. I had been preparing for months, running, climbing, lifting, pushing my lean, wiry body to the limit. On one occasion, one of the older recruits called me a "stripling." I smiled, and then kicked him hard enough to drop him to the sand. No one called me names after that.

After I received the news that I had passed, I went to my Captain and asked to see my sister.

"You have completed your first stage of training," he said. "You may visit your sister."

I'll never forget the relief that washed over me when I saw Salina—Silva, as she was now known. She looked healthy, having grown quite a lot in the four years we had been apart. She was overjoyed to see me...almost too much so. Something nagged at the back of my mind when I looked at her hands. They were roughened and red, the nails ragged. *She has been biting them, tearing at them hard enough to make her fingers bleed.*

"What happened to your hands?" I asked.

She quickly thrust them beneath the folds of her

garment. "Nothing…they're just rough from the work I do."

"And what work is that?" I asked, unsure of how a ten-year-old girl could work hard enough to make her fingers bleed.

"Oh, you know…I do a lot of washing and cleaning. We girls aren't taught the same lessons as you. Anyway, the Headmistress has told me I should take better care of my hands. She says I'll never get a husband otherwise."

"Well, at least all the men will know what a hard worker you are," I said, trying to cheer her, but the dread in her eyes made the hair on the back of my neck stand up. I shivered, trying to banish the chill that had come over me. Salina threw her arms around me, shaking. "Let's go home, Glennroy. We need to go back home…before this place changes us too much," she said. "There's no Sickness anymore."

I didn't know what to do. "We can't go home," I whispered. "Be quiet, now…they won't like it if they hear you say such things. Haven't you taken the Oath? I know I did. We can't leave."

She drew back, her wise, round eyes fixed on mine. "I asked for you every day."

I felt a lump rising in my throat. "I asked about you, too. But they wouldn't let us be together until I completed my training." Even as I said the words, I knew how lame they sounded. I should have found a way. I had promised my father I would protect her. The thought made me cross. "Anyway, this is our home now, and we should make the most of it. Just try to be content, will you? One day you'll marry a fine man, and have a house full of children. You'll be happy…I just know it."

She cast her gaze down to her feet. "I still have the dreams. You might hope for happiness, and you might have it, but not with hearth and home…not here. I don't see that future for either of us." Then she closed her eyes. "Maybe you shouldn't come here anymore."

I stared at her. "But why?"

"Because it will make us both sad."

I gripped her arm. "I promised Father that I would look after you, and I intend to. I won't hear any argument from you."

Her eyelashes, wet with tears, fluttered up at me. "I can look after myself. You have to let me do that, and follow your own path. Just try to keep your heart open a little bit. The world—bad people—will try to close it. Goodbye, Glennroy. I will love you always."

When had she gotten so…*old?* I stood in shock as I realized she meant every word—she would not allow another visit from me. I couldn't think of anything to say, but could only watch as she composed herself, clasped my hands once more with her ragged fingers, and then turned to leave me alone in the room.

***

My training was far from over.

At first, I was treated the same as any other new recruit. I was happy to be free of daily classroom lessons, and eventually I settled into my new routine with hardly a thought given to Salina and her ominous words. We were given assignments every day—sometimes we were sent to dig a well or repair a wall, but mostly we just sparred with one another and played at mock battles. Unfortunately, Jamar and two of his companions had been assigned to my Company. They tried to make things difficult for me whenever the Captain wasn't looking. That was when I discovered my particular talent for disappearing.

Sometimes, if a recruit received a special assignment, it was given to him on a slip of paper. It might mean anything—polish the officers' boots, exercise the horses, take blades to the smithy to be sharpened—and I received my share of tasks.

I stayed in this routine for four more years, during which time I refined some of my skills, worked hard at menial tasks, and tried not to run afoul of Jamar and his associates. For the most part I was content, though there was something missing. Now that I was an official recruit, they had given my father's axe back to me. I remember looking into its polished surface, observing the lean, scruffy-bearded face of the young man staring back at me. *Is there anything more?* I asked myself. *Will I ever achieve greatness? I don't care about being happy…I want to be important enough that I won't need to hide from people like Jamar. And…I want to make a difference, too. King Darius is called "The Just." If I serve him, perhaps I can prevent the stupid, fearful people from doing harm to innocents like my father and brother.*

I had never seen King Darius. From what I heard, few people ever had. But he and his Gleaners had rescued Salina and me, and that was enough to earn my loyalty.

One day I received my assignment as usual, but it was the first time I had ever seen the word "ministry" printed there. That meant my presence was required in front of one or more of the City's ministers—the advisors who carried out the orders of the King.

The Ministry was quite a change from my austere quarters—hung with tapestries and set with water-fountains that sparkled in the sunlight filtering down through panels in the ceiling. I wondered how they worked—what made the water flow. I sat obediently in an elaborately carved chair, trying to imagine what they could possibly want with me.

Three ministers came into the room, along with four enormous, fierce-looking guards. *Why would they need guards? Especially armed with great axes—they look more like executioners.* All my nerve endings were tingling as I rose to my feet.

"Please sit down," said one of the ministers. "You can relax…you've done nothing wrong as yet." Two of the axe-carrying guards stood behind the chair on either side.

Well, now I can certainly relax.

I looked at the ministers, trying to imagine what would come next. The one in the center, a short, rather stocky man with penetrating grey eyes, spoke first. His voice was soothing, melodic—almost hypnotic.

Careful…

"I'm sure you wonder why we have called you here. It's Beltran, isn't it?"

"Yes, my lords. Beltran."

"We have come to make you an offer, Beltran. You have an extraordinary amount of potential, and, to be honest, the King needs men like you. But I must warn you—we do not make this offer lightly. Once we have made it, you will only have two choices. One is to accept the honor your King would bestow. The other is to lose the King's favor."

He paused for a moment, allowing the impact of his words to sink in, as one of his companions stepped forward. "You may leave now with no penalty," he said. "But if you stay, you either leave as a member of a very elite group, or with dishonor."

I thought I knew what he meant by that—they would carry me out feet first.

"Let's be plain," I said. "If I refuse, I will meet with the wrong end of an axe. Isn't that what you really intend?" To their credit, they barely registered any surprise at the question.

"I see you have a good grasp of your situation," said the first. "If you refuse the wishes of King Darius, you must be treated as an enemy to the Crown."

"We will, of course, bury you with full honors," said the third. "No one else will know of your dishonor."

Ah. Now I feel ever so much better. What in the world have I gotten myself into?

"If you accept, you will be taken into a very select fraternity with a long and glorious tradition," said the first.

"May I ask a question?" I said, shifting in my seat.

"You may ask," said the second, "though we may not answer."

"Which of my abilities, precisely, caused you to select me for this honor?"

They whispered briefly to one another. "We will not say until you decide whether to hear our offer," said the first. "You may leave now if you'd like. However, we must ask you not to speak of this meeting if you do. If we hear otherwise, you will not live long, I assure you."

They stood patiently for a moment or two as I considered. "We had thought you to be a decisive young man," said the first. "Now shall we escort you back to your quarters, or will you stay and hear what we have to tell?"

I didn't trust them to have anyone escort me back—at least not alive. "Is this...occupation...more interesting than my current one?" I asked. "Because, to be frank, there has been very little to interest me in my present one."

"Oh, I can assure you, it is interesting," said the second. "Perhaps the greatest challenge a man like you can face."

A man like me? What does he mean?

I knew I could not leave without hearing what they had to offer. Curiosity is one of my more troublesome character flaws. "All right," I said. "Make your offer."

***

I did not return to my barracks—I had my own quarters after that. I was told that I would train with a Mentor every day, and I would be well cared for. In return, all I had to be able to do was keep to myself. I would be allowed to go abroad in the City, but I was advised to form no attachments—make no friends, in other words—and I could not speak of my profession to anyone, not even my sister. In fact, I was forbidden to see Salina.

"If you accept our offer, you will have no family from now on," said the Ministers. I had felt a pang of doubt. *Give up ever seeing my sister? Surely they will relent.* Besides…Salina had so much as told me she didn't want to see me.

One of the Ministers must have anticipated my momentary reluctance, but he knew just what to say to convince me. "You will serve the King in the highest capacity possible. You will be one who removes his fears, safeguards the City from her deadliest enemies, and promotes justice and peace. There is no higher calling in Orovar."

I recall the swelling of pride in my chest when I heard those words. *Me. They have chosen me!* Pride overwhelmed duty, and I brushed my sister aside. All I wanted, from that day forward, was to serve the King. I wanted to become a shadow-man.

***

The first time I met my Mentor, I wondered what I had gotten myself into. I had been languishing happily on the soft blue velvet couch in my new quarters when he simply appeared standing next to me. Dressed entirely in grey, it was as though he had formed from the shadows themselves. He had made no sound.

"Hello, Beltran. My name is Corvyn, but you will address me as 'Master' from now on. I will be your only companion—the only one in whom you may confide, anyway. How much have they told you?"

"How did you get in here without my knowing it?"

"I'll ask the questions," he said. "How much have they told you?"

"Only that I have been chosen to serve King Darius, and that I may not reveal my profession to anyone. I have been expecting you. They told me I would train with a Mentor." I looked him up and down, from his steely eyes to his soft-booted feet.

"You think me ordinary. I can see it in your expression," he said with a slight smile. "Never mind. You'll soon learn otherwise."

"I don't think you ordinary at all. You sneaked in here without a sound. Most people can't surprise me the way you did."

He laughed. "Well, good. That's the first step. It's my job to teach you how to remain unseen and unheard. I'm getting older, and it's time for me to mentor the next in line. If you pass all my tests, it will be you."

"And what if I don't pass them?"

"We shouldn't speak of such things now," he said.

"But…" I started to protest, but the only thing I remember after that is lying paralyzed on the floor, trying to breathe. I had no idea what Corvyn had done to me,

The Shadow-Man

but it had been wicked fast and reasonably painful.

"That's how you immobilize a man without giving him a chance to speak," said Corvyn. "I can show you how to do that, and I will, but you must follow every order I give you. You may neither argue nor protest. Is that clear?"

The only sound I could make was a feeble "aahhhhhhh."

"Oh, very well. Nod if you can."

I did.

"Very good," said Corvyn, drawing a blade from beneath the folds of his robe. He looked down at me with an expression of pure disdain. "Oh, for heaven's sake, don't worry. I won't hurt you yet. It's my job to train you, not kill you." He began cleaning his nails with the point of the blade. "First, I'll show you how to surprise a man. Then, how to render him helpless. Finally, I'll teach you to kill." With those words, he replaced his blade. "We start tomorrow."

I closed my eyes and nodded. When I opened them again, he was gone. As the feeling began to come back to my arms and legs, I was aware of three things: that my body was most unhappy, that I hated my new mentor, and that I wanted to be just like him.

***

I trained with Corvyn each day. It was a real exercise in discipline for me, as I dared not ever speak without permission. Other than "yes, Master," or "no, Master," I said very little. Occasionally I forgot myself, to my great regret. Corvyn made a mark on me for every transgression—just a little scratch with the tip of his blade—saying that the day I bore no mark, I would be rewarded. This would prove to be a lot harder than it sounded. It meant that I could not acquire any new marks for the length of time required to heal the old ones.

Then, one day, he appeared at the corner table near my balcony, a big tray of very fine food and wine balanced on one hand. "It seems you bear no mark today," he said, smiling. "As promised, you may have your reward. There will be no training today." He set the tray down on the table. Eat, drink, and enjoy your leisure time," he said. "Tomorrow we start afresh…and I believe you'll find this new level somewhat taxing. However, the rest of your reward will be here after sundown."

I bowed. "Yes, Master."

Corvyn chuckled. "You may speak freely for now," he said.

I drew a deep breath, eyeing the delicacies on the tray with anticipation. They had fed me well enough, but with little consideration of my palate. "Thank you, Master," I said, and meant it.

"You've earned it," he replied. "As for the rest of your reward, well…I have a very special token for you." He drew close, reaching under his robe again. I was always amazed by the quantity and variety of items he could conceal there. This time he drew forth a small bottle made of blue glass. "If you experience any feelings of…shyness…tonight, drink this. You'll feel no fear."

I took the bottle. "Fear? What should I fear?" I asked.

"I'm not saying you will, but just in case you do," he said. "Goodnight, Beltran. Save some of your strength for tomorrow."

That evening, at sundown, I understood what he meant. I had gone out into the City to take the air, and when I returned there was someone else in my chamber. She was the most beautiful woman I had ever beheld. I swallowed hard, realizing what she was there for…a thing

The Shadow-Man

I had never done before. Almost without thinking, I reached into my pocket, drew forth the little blue bottle, and swallowed every drop of the liquid fire inside it.

From that day on, I was given women whenever I asked for them—provided Corvyn allowed it. He would allow it whenever I performed well in training, which was nearly every session.

"You have mastered the art of stealth, and you have become formidable," he said. "Now it is time to learn to kill."

"I already know how to do that," I said. "I killed a man when I was eleven."

Corvyn shook his head. "Anyone can kill like a beast, hacking and stabbing and bludgeoning. You will learn the *art* of murder—to kill so that no one suspects malfeasance. You will be like the small grey spider that bites, kills, and leaves unnoticed. Your victims will be assumed to have died naturally, or by their own hand. This is difficult—and very important!"

"How does such a skill serve the King?" I asked.

"Because if you succeed, you will become a shadow-man. It will be your job to make certain the King's enemies—enemies of peace and justice—are no longer there to threaten the City. And you must do it without bringing suspicion upon the King. All your prior training has led to this very specialized duty. Has it really taken you so long to realize this?"

"You're a shadow-man, aren't you? How many people have you killed?" I asked.

"As many as required of me and no more. A shadow-man does not ask "why." He simply does his duty according to his training. I swear a very special oath each day—one which confirms my devotion to the King and commitment to my duty. Should you prove worthy, you will swear the same oath. You have acquitted yourself well in your training so far. Today we begin to find out whether you are truly worthy."

Corvyn taught me many things. I could not possibly recount all of them, but the rest of my tale requires that I reveal at least a few of our secrets. By the time I was ready for my first real test, I had learned how to paralyze a man by striking him in a certain spot, I could stop the flow of blood to his brain without leaving a mark on him, and I could use any one of a number of poisons that would kill quickly or slowly, but would mimic other illness such as afflictions of the heart and lungs, or the bowels and blood. We had physicians in the City, of course, but they would labor in vain. Corvyn's poisons were undeniably lethal.

"Do you think you can kill a man?" he asked me one day after a particularly gruesome demonstration of a suffocating technique. He used animals, usually monkeys, for such demonstrations, and this one had not gone quietly.

"I would rather they not resist so much," I said, shuddering at the memory of the monkey's terrified, rolling eyes.

"Of course you wouldn't. Here's how you do it with finesse." Corvyn led me to a darkened chamber and gently drew the cover from a large cage. A second monkey, curled up in a pile of blankets, was fast asleep.

"Don't worry," said Corvyn. "This one won't wake up easily. I've given it a sleeping-draught. Now…first, you must ensure your victim feels nothing." He carefully opened the cage door. Then he reached inside, a dropper in his gloved right hand, and squeezed a small amount of liquid into the monkey's mouth.

The animal's breathing quickened, and it licked its lips, but did not awaken. Another few moments and its eyelids sagged open. "See how glassy-eyed it is?" said Corvyn. "It's ready to kill." He drew forth a small pillow—a special one filled with a jelly-like material made from seaweed—and pressed it over the monkey's face. Other than a brief stiffening of the monkey's limbs, there was no struggle. The body went flaccid after a couple of minutes. "There," said Corvyn. "It's done. Now, wasn't that better?"

"I have to agree," I said, looking at the now-dead animal in wonder.

"You can arrange for people to literally die peacefully in their beds if you so choose. But you can only use this method when you're sure you will have the time to carry it out. Usually it's just safer to introduce a poison and leave. Now, I'll ask again…are you ready to kill?"

"Yes," I said. "I believe I am." Such an easy thing to say.

Corvyn withdrew the monkey from the cage and handed it to me. "Get rid of that, will you? Tomorrow, we'll see."

***

I spent the whole next day wondering what Corvyn meant by "we'll see." By the time he appeared, twilight had fallen over the tall towers of Orovar, including mine. I recall standing and looking out over the dusky horizon when my mentor appeared beside me. I jumped in spite of myself.

"Sorry," I muttered. "I should be used to your comings and goings by now."

"Woe befalls the day I can't startle an apprentice," he said, looking me up and down. "You're sweating. You've been fretting all day, haven't you?" There was just a little contempt in the smile he wore.

"Yes, I have been fretting, and one can hardly blame me, what with your mysterious, doom-laden pronouncements. Now, what is it that you want, Master? This day is nearly over."

Corvyn chuckled. "Yes, yes, it is nearly over. But the night is just beginning, and it will be long. Shadow-men work in darkness, Beltran. It's time you went to work."

He reached into his robes and brought out a small slip of paper. I took it, examining the words printed there. "Eldric the Traitor? Who is Eldric the Traitor?" I asked.

"The man you are going to kill tonight. If you succeed, you will have proven your worth to the King," said Corvyn. I will tell you of his crime, and where you may find him, but nothing more. Do not return until your task is done."

Standing there, holding the paper with the doomed man's name on it, I felt the blood drain from my face. My training had led to this, as I had known it would, but it was…it was so soon. *Can I do this? Do I have the strength?*

Corvyn, who was quite possibly the most perceptive man I have ever met, put a strong hand on my shoulder. I glanced over at it, wondering how many lives he had taken with his strong hands. "Eldric's crime is treason," he said. "The traitor has plotted to overthrow good King Darius and take the throne for himself. Now, does that help you?"

I nodded, swallowing hard.

"Good. I'll leave you to it, then. You will find Eldric in the fourth chamber on the third level of the Ministers' Tower, at least I expect you will. He is usually there after nightfall. Here is the elixir you will need." He handed me a small phial of amber-colored fluid. "This will stop his

The Shadow-Man

heart. It will appear as though he has died naturally. Make sure you give him all of it." He turned to leave, but turned back just before he disappeared into the shadows. "Remember, Beltran—you must not fail. Once the elixir starts to take effect, get out of there. Don't wait. If you are discovered, it is *you* who will be branded a traitor. No one will even claim to know your name. Do you understand?"

"I understand. But, Master…if Eldric is a traitor, why don't they just lop off his head in the City Square? Why send me?"

"A shadow-man does not question! He obeys the King's commands," said Corvyn with a steely edge to his voice.

"But I am not a shadow-man yet," I said.

"You're right. Very well, then…there are those who would not agree with executing Eldric, and they have power. It's better this way. You know nothing of the affairs of the King—it's not our business to know. If you cannot grasp that simple truth, then all my efforts will have been in vain."

I didn't care for the look in his eyes, and I knew I was in peril. Though I believed Corvyn had developed some fondness for me, I realized that he would kill me without a word. I had to say something, and it had to be right. "I understand, Master."

To my relief, his gaze softened. "Now, go on and do what you have been trained to do," he said. "I will wait for you. And remember—leave no mark!"

***

I had not realized how formidable my job would be. It's a lot easier when there's nothing at stake. I remember crouching in the shadows near the Ministers' Tower, gazing up at the window of the fourth chamber, third level. Inside lay my victim, or so I hoped. Perhaps he would already be asleep. If not, I would lurk and wait until the time was right. I thought I knew how to get in—there was a ledge between the window and the balcony on the third level—but it wouldn't be as easy as it had been in training.

A short while later, I had managed to scale the wall to the third level using a hook and cord. I gave thanks for the moonless night as I worked my way from the balcony to Eldric's window-ledge. Once there, I used a small hand-mirror to peer inside without showing my face. A man, presumably Eldric the Traitor, lay in his bed, an open book on his chest. I was in luck—I could hear him snoring softly. Now to open the window…

Drat! It's locked! Now what? I remembered the small metal tool Corvyn had given me. With a bit of skill, one could open most doors with it, but windows were another matter. They only had locks on the inside. I couldn't break the window or use a cutting tool—the death had to appear natural.

I would have to use the door. That meant sneaking in to the Ministers' Tower, which was always heavily guarded, and then contending with the undoubtedly locked door to Eldric's chamber. I glanced down at the second level. There was one open window, and I would make for it. I worked my way down, gloved hands on the slender cord that was my life-line, and balanced precariously on the window-ledge.

Inside I saw a man and woman, apparently asleep, an empty wine-bottle on the floor beside the bed. I slipped in, crept to the door, and stood there for a few moments. How would I get out of here and get up to the fourth chamber without being seen? There were sure to be

The Shadow-Man

guards, weren't there? I needed a diversion.

I noticed a half-full bottle of spirits on the table, and I knew what I would do. I moved to the window, doused the draperies with spirits, and set them aflame, hoping to arouse the sleeping man and woman, who would then raise an alarm. I would easily get lost in the confusion and encounter no difficulty getting up to Eldric's chamber. I waited near the door, knowing I would escape as soon as anyone opened it.

I had underestimated the amount of wine the man and woman had consumed, for they didn't even stir, but someone obviously saw smoke billowing from the window—I heard the alarm bells ring. The Tower was soon in relative chaos. When some men burst in to put out the fire, I left the chamber unnoticed, made my way to the third level, and hid in the shadows. I saw a man in a dressing-gown emerge from Eldric's chamber, obviously distressed by the clamor.

"What's all the noise? Is there a danger?" he asked, grabbing a passing guard by the arm.

"No, Minister...no danger, just a small fire on the second level. We're making certain all is secure. You may go back to your bed. There's nothing to fear."

Eldric's eyes narrowed. "What caused the fire?"

"Spilled liquor appears to be involved," said the guard with a wink. "I'm sure you can probably guess who might have spilled it."

"Ah. Yes, I probably can. When are they going to remove all the flammables from Deputy-minister Pascal's chamber? At least as long as his drunken wife is still with him..."

"Indeed," said the guard, chuckling. "You might bring it up in the next Council-meeting. Sleep well, Minister."

Once Eldric had gone back inside, I waited long

enough for him to have fallen asleep again. This time I knew I could get inside, as I had my tool and I knew how to use it. Then the most difficult part of my task would begin.

I stood beside the bed, watching the sleeping man. The regular rise and fall of his chest, the gentle sounds of sleep coming from his half-open mouth, the slight fluttering of his eyelids—all bore testimony to the life within. He looked healthy, though he was not a young man. The elixir, Corvyn had said, would stop his heart.

There was no way to do this peacefully, as I would have to get him to swallow the entire contents of the phial. To do that, I would have to stop his mouth and nose after pouring the elixir in. He would have no choice but to swallow it. I readied myself, knowing I would be in for at least a brief struggle, as I took the cork from the phial.

Who is this man? Why does he deserve to die?

I shook my head, trying to banish such thoughts, as I could not afford them. *A shadow-man does not ask questions. I must trust the King...Good King Darius, the man I owe my life to, though I have never seen him. If not for him, we would have been lost...lost to the Moon Man and the other mindless, superstitious monsters who burned my brother alive.*

I looked at the sleeping man, imagining the face of one of the villagers who had no doubt lit many a pyre. The torch light had revealed his insanity...his stupid, unreasonable fear. Without another thought, I grabbed the man's jaw and poured the elixir into his mouth, then sat astride his chest, pinching his nostrils shut and covering his mouth with a grey-gloved hand as he struggled awake.

I ignored the terror in his eyes as he bucked and heaved underneath me. I stopped looking at his face when his eyes rolled back in his head and he went limp. Unfortunately, at that moment, someone knocked at the door. *Get out of there. Don't wait...*

I wanted to check my victim for a heart-beat, but there wasn't time. I flew to the window, unlocked it, and eased myself outside. Despite Corvyn's instructions, I wanted to make sure—to follow the kill until there was no doubt of it—and so I waited. I heard someone unlock the chamber door. Then I heard that someone trying to rouse the minister. Cautiously, I peered inside.

Eldric the Traitor lay where I had left him, but someone had drawn a cloth over his face. I knew what that meant—I had succeeded. I had become a shadow-man.

✷✷✷

I returned to my chamber to find Corvyn waiting for me. "You didn't tell me he would struggle so hard," I said. "Still, the deed is done. I killed him. Next time, I'd rather use a less painful method, even if he was a traitor."

"The struggle was necessary," said Corvyn. "I had to test you thoroughly. You have to be willing not only to kill a stranger, but to cause him pain. Congratulations. I must say, though…your diversion was more than a little clumsy. I'm not sure why you needed one, anyway. You got into Pascal's chamber…why didn't you just spirit yourself up to the third level without setting the place on fire? It wouldn't do to burn the Tower down."

"There was little risk of that," I said, though I couldn't look Corvyn in the eye at that point. He was right, as usual.

"Wasn't there?"

"No one will suspect wrong-doing. The wife has a

problem with drink. I heard the guard say so."

"Actually, Pascal has more of a drinking problem than the wife does, and you should know the guard works for me," said Corvyn. "Those words were spoken for your benefit. Eldric, who is not a traitor, was in on the test, too. I hope you didn't actually damage him during the struggle."

I just stood with my mouth open.

"You didn't think we would entrust such a vital task to an untested assassin, would you? Our work is far too important to risk in the hands of an apprentice. The elixir I gave you was of excellent quality, but not lethal in any way. Eldric is a fine actor, don't you agree?"

I stood before him, clenching and unclenching my hands, wanting to throttle him.

"Don't be angry, Beltran. We are all tested this way. Some people just can't take a life no matter how much you train them. When the time comes, their courage deserts them. I'm pleased that you passed my last test."

"I told you I had killed a man already," I said through clenched teeth.

"Yes, a man who was about to attack you and your sister. You told me all about it. This time wasn't so easy, was it? Eldric wasn't threatening you. He had no power over you—he was asleep in his bed. That was a much greater test of your resolve, don't you think? Now, it's nearly dawn, so get some rest. Tonight we'll go and meet Eldric. I want to get his evaluation of your performance in his untimely demise."

After Corvyn had left, my thoughts turned back to the murder I thought I had committed. It hadn't been all that difficult, really...not once I had talked myself into it. I knew I could do it again, and this time I wouldn't ask questions. I would trust King Darius to know when and where he needed my services, and I would provide those services. I knew I could practice the art of killing, and that I would refine it with each life taken. As long as I could wall off the part of my soul that worried about whether it was right or wrong, I would be fine.

***

Corvyn and I made our way to the *Boar's Head* tavern later that night. Sure enough, there was Eldric sitting in a corner booth—our booth. One could see everyone who came in the front door (and the back door) from that shadowy corner. It was always dark in the *Boar's Head*, but I could see that Eldric had already ordered a huge platter of corn-battered onions fried in lard. As usual, the whole place smelled of onions and stale beer. I loved it.

Corvyn clapped him on the shoulder. "You're looking remarkably hale for a dead man."

"No thanks to you," said Eldric with a rather jaundiced look in my direction. "Your protégé nearly smothered the life out of me."

Corvyn shrugged. "Hazard of the job. Besides, Abiel was there to make sure things didn't go too far. We wouldn't have let him kill you...not really."

"Well, this is the last time, I hope," said Eldric. "What if he had decided to break my neck instead?"

"He's smarter than that," said Corvyn.

"What say we stop talking about him as if he isn't here?" I said, somewhat annoyed at having been cast in the role of "the-only-one-who-didn't-know-what-was-going-on."

"At least your elixir was of a better vintage than the last," said Eldric.

"Wine?" I muttered. "You had me risk my life to pour

wine down his throat? *Wine?*"

"Yes, and very fine wine, too," said Eldric. "Though it wasn't really worth the bruise you put on my chin when you held me down." He turned back to Corvyn. "I was almost worried there for a moment."

Corvyn leaned in, picked up the lone candle from the center of the scarred mahogany table, and held it near Eldric's face. "You did leave a bruise, though it's a small one and likely would not have aroused suspicion. You must do better the next time. For now, though, let's drink to your success. What say you, Eldric? Did he pass?"

"I suppose so. He definitely would have killed me had your elixir been genuine." He lifted his hardwood tankard in my direction and took a long swallow, foam bubbling in his grey mustache. "Here's to your apprentice, Corvyn. I hope to never meet up with him again…at least not anywhere but here."

A full tankard was placed at my elbow, and I drank it down in my own honor. "Don't be too impressed with yourself," said Corvyn. "The next time you're called upon, you'll be on your own, and it will be real."

***

I went to the tavern nearly every night after that, and the proprietor, a rather smallish, rat-faced man named Hakim, made certain I could sit in my usual corner. Sometimes I envied him—he had what I considered to be an ideal profession, though I suspected it would neither be challenging enough nor profitable enough to suit me.

As a shadow-man, I was treated very well. I had women whenever I asked for them, though never the same one twice, and I was given every comfort—spending money, food, drink, and fine clothes. My whip-thin, sinewy frame and raven-black hair might be considered handsome, and some folk thought me quite dashing, especially when I dressed up in tailored leathers, silks, and velvets. I must admit that I soon became very impressed with myself in general, though I always wore old clothes to the tavern. When asked how I made my living, I merely replied that I was a part of the King's personal guard. That was true enough.

"And how did you merit such an honor?" snarled one of the other regulars.

"Apparently, the King values my skills," I said, demonstrating by casting one of my throwing-knives just past his ear to stick in the wall with a solid *thunk*. "Now, I would suggest you not question me again."

The man shrugged. "Fair enough. Still, you must have seen the King, eh? Tell me...what's he like?"

"Kingly," I replied, downing a small jolt of strong spirits. "If he wanted you to know more, he would tell you himself."

Even as I said the words, I wondered. I had never seen King Darius, and neither had anyone else of my acquaintance. He didn't appear to address his subjects—his words were read by the First Minister, always emphasizing how much the King loved his people and how every law, every edict, was made for their protection and prosperity. Why did he not appear? What did he fear? Sometimes I wondered whether he existed at all.

I embraced my new profession, though I was rarely called upon at first. My shadow fell across only three souls the first year, and I looked forward to each challenge knowing I was eliminating an enemy of the Crown.

My assignments always arrived with a meal, usually hidden beneath the cap of my wine-bottle. Bottles containing messages were always dipped in red wax...an uncommon practice in the city. To this day, I shy away from bottles like that. I was told why each "mark" had been selected for my attentions. For example, a message would read: *Trask, a traitor who has plotted to poison the King's wine. We could not catch him red-handed, and thus cannot accuse him openly, but we are certain of his guilt. The shadow must fall upon him.* I was told where and when Trask could be found. Then I would burn the message.

I told myself that each killing was justified, though it really didn't matter. A shadow-man doesn't ask questions. Today I wonder how much of those justifications were true. Was Trask really a traitor? Did the woman named Bint Falina really conspire to murder Darius's favorite consort? At one point it seemed I was called upon to eliminate the leading members of a certain religious sect. When I asked Corvyn about it, he dismissed it as coincidence. In Orovar, anyone breaking the law was supposed to be put on trial in the City Court. Though they were usually then found guilty, I'm quite certain none of my victims were ever granted such a courtesy.

Sometimes I was sent to the neighboring guild-villages to practice the shadow-man's very special way of settling disputes over taxes, labor conditions, and duties owed to the Crown, though, naturally, I was told otherwise. My victims were always described as the worst sort of conspirators, always on the verge of major rebellion that would plunge Orovar into chaos. I was generally content with my lot in life, and therefore I did what I was told without investigating the truth of it. My father would have wept at what I had become, but I hadn't thought of him in a long, long time. I couldn't even remember what he looked like—at least not while he was alive.

As the years passed, and I was called upon more and more often, I began to wonder. For one thing, the assignments had been reduced to a simple name and location, with no explanation or justification provided. I had perfected the technique of stupefying my victims with moon-flower and then suffocating them, but I wondered how much longer things could go on before people began to wonder why so many of Darius' enemies died in their beds.

Though I still trained and disciplined myself in order to stay strong and hardy, my relatively easy life had lost much of its appeal. I began to entertain thoughts of pursuing a different way of earning a living. I was still a relatively young man, and I grew tired of keeping to myself all the time. Fine food and female company only provide so much personal fulfillment. I remember looking at my unshaven face in the glass in my quarters. Who was that bored, hard-eyed man staring back at me?

I started taking risks for no good reason, and it's a miracle I wasn't caught. The only other exciting moments in my life came during my nightly visits to the *Boar's Head*, where I could find a few hours of companionship and mayhem with the few people I had come to know. They called me "El-morah," which refers to a water-hole that looks good but is undrinkable, as if they knew there was something unsavory beneath the fair surface. I believe they were pointing out that, while I called myself a "King's Man," I was generally worthless.

Since I always had plenty of money and wasn't shy about spreading it around, no one objected too much—not even Jamar, who had taken to coming in on a regular basis. I noticed he had working man's hands and the beginnings of a gut hanging over his belt. It was obvious that he was no longer in the military, and I wondered what he had done to bring dishonor on himself. He wisely avoided me.

I had achieved status while my old enemy had been humbled, and that realization re-kindled my appreciation of the life I had chosen. Fueled by pride, I carried out two more executions before my day of reckoning finally came.

***

The message hidden beneath the red wax cork of the wine bottle simply read "Martell the Wise. Scholars' Keep, Lore-master's quarters." I stared at it for a moment. I had actually met Martell—he was one of the King's closest and most trusted advisors, the Chief Lore-master in Orovar. This would be a very high-level assassination involving one of the highest-ranking citizens. Martell had seemed very kind, gentle, almost grandfatherly, though I heard he could be quite caustic if you were apprenticed to him. He would not suffer a fool.

I prepared everything I would need…moon-flower, the special mask I used for smothering people, and all the tools I would need to break into the Scholars' Keep. As it turned out, I didn't need them. Scholars, apparently, didn't bother to lock their doors at night. The underground vault containing the City's library, however, was locked, as was the Lore-master's quarters. As it was locked from the inside, and I had no way of getting in other than through the door, I would need to wait a while.

Each evening I made my way to the Keep, hoping that someone would decide to visit Martell and give me an opportunity. Finally, on the third evening of lurking, a robed, hooded apprentice appeared with a tray of food and wine. He knocked softly at the heavy oaken door.

"Master…I have brought a late supper as you requested."

I heard a voice from within the chamber, though not clearly. Then the rattling of the lock…the turning of the

The Shadow-Man

key. "Come in, my son," said a kindly voice. "Pray take some supper with a lonely old man." The apprentice entered the room, but he left the door ajar—the opportunity I had been waiting for.

Now just relax and get into some discussion about something or other, I thought. *Take your attentions elsewhere for a few moments—that's all I need.* I slipped into the chamber and hid beneath the cloth covering one of Martell's study-tables as the two scholars—young and old—shared the food and wine on the tray.

When they had finished, Martell drew out a carved wooden pipe, filled it with leaf, and touched it to the candle-flame. Soon he was puffing away, though the smoke made him cough rather alarmingly. I could not see the apprentice clearly, as he was still hooded, but he rose and moved to pat Martell on the back to help him stop coughing. Martell waved him away.

From the sound of it, you'll need a lot more than a pat on the back, I thought. *But soon it won't matter anyway. Enjoy your pipe, old man.*

At last, the apprentice gathered up the tray. "Goodnight, Master. Sleep well," he said, and left me alone with Martell.

It was a good thing Martell had drunk as much wine as he had, or he might never have gone to sleep at all. I knew that Lore-masters often loved to work far into the night, and that old men sometimes don't seem to need to sleep much, but I was hoping to complete my task and get back to my quarters. Staying absolutely quiet and motionless for such a long time tired me out like nothing else could...in fact, I doubt I could do it today. Whether Martell needed sleep or not, I most certainly would.

At last he stretched, yawned, and moved to his bedchamber. A moment later, the lamp went out. I waited a few more moments, and crept quietly in. The room was so dark I could barely see Martell, as there were no windows and precious little light from the study-chamber, but back then I had cat's eyes. I moved unerringly to the bedside, the phial of moon-flower in my hand. I had crouched beside the bed and was preparing to administer the elixir—just a few drops would do the trick—when I heard the old man speak.

"I've been wondering when Darius would decide to include me in his unending list of enemies."

This had never happened to me in all my years. I had never been anticipated before, at least, not as far as I knew. What could I do now? I knew I could overpower Martell, but not without leaving evidence.

"Well, get on with it. I know who you are, and why you've come. You will make it painless, won't you?"

I didn't know what to say. When I tried to speak, my words came out rough and halting, as though I hadn't used my voice in a long time. "I...I can make it so you will not suffer," I said. "But why do you give in so easily? Why not fight for your life? Is it worth so little to you?"

"On the contrary. My life is worth a great deal to me," said Martell, reaching over to the bedside table. "Light that candle, will you? In my opinion, you should at least have the courtesy to look me in the eye before you kill me."

I obliged him...what else could I do? I looked into his watery blue eyes—the eyes of a Northerner—as he peered back at me. "Drat. It's so difficult to see without lenses," he said. "Never mind...you asked me why I don't fight. Do you still want to know? Well, of course you do. I'll wager you've never had one of your targets speak for itself before." He drew a deep, resigned sigh. "I don't fight because there's no point. I've spent most of my life in Orovar, serving the City. When Darius came, I served him as well...I have been there for him through all of his difficulties, and I have kept his secrets. If he has sent you after me, I can do nothing more to aid him. That means my life is over, whether by your hand or someone else's."

"If he has sent me, you are an enemy to the Crown," I said. "What do you mean by keeping the King's secrets? You must not have kept them very well, not if he mistrusts you enough to order a visit from me."

"He trusts no one," said Martell. "Did you not know it?" His eyes widened, and he shook his head. "You really don't know, do you? You're in the employ of a madman. Darius has not been of sound mind for many years now...you have been doing the bidding of a man who has not known who his friends are for quite a long while. I don't know whether it matters to you, but you have probably been killing innocent people since you came into your profession."

"I don't believe you," I said, still having trouble finding my voice. "You're just trying to talk your way out of your difficulty."

Martell laughed. "What's that in your hand? Moon-flower? What were you going to do, render me insensible and then smother me, I suppose. Just like so many others...but this time you have to listen to what I have to say first. Now, if you still believe I'm trying to talk you out of it, I'll say this once more—I'm a doomed man, and I know it. I'd rather be spared the humiliation of a public execution. If you'll hand over the phial, I'll go quietly."

I hesitated. "Oh, don't worry," he said. "You can still overpower me, and I know it." He took the phial from my nerveless right hand. "I will say only one thing more, Shadow-man. You've never seen King Darius, have you? Yet you are in his employ. Try to get in to see him—and not through official channels, as you will never be admitted. No...you will need to gain entrance like the shadow-man you are. Once you have seen the King, you will have another decision to make. Here's hoping it will be the right one."

With those words, he flipped the cork from the phial with his thumb and drank the entire contents down in one swallow. "Ah. That feels wonderful going down...like, like a gentle flash of bright light that...does...not...burn. Most...curious." He sagged over, his eyes still open, and I knew he would stop breathing soon enough, but I still held the mask over his face until the life drained out of him. That way I wouldn't have to look at his dying eyes.

Afterward, I tended Martell's body, arranging his coverlet and closing his eyes. He had been worthy of respect. I just sat beside him for a few moments, until I heard the knock at the door.

"Master? Are you awake?" said a voice. "I have your breakfast." It sounded like the apprentice. To my dismay, I realized that Martell had kept me until nearly dawn. The apprentice knocked louder. "Master! I have breakfast. Are you all right?"

He wasn't giving up. Now what? Well, I could always set the place on fire and escape in the confusion. The old man smoked, after all...it seemed as good a chance as any. They would break the door down, and I could escape. But what if they didn't? What if I was overcome by smoke first? Then they would find me. Quietly I crept to the door, turned the bolt, and shrank back in the shadows against the wall. When the apprentice entered with the breakfast tray, he looked puzzled. No wonder—he was expecting the old man. I knew I should wait...let him take a few more steps inside, perhaps move to the table to set down the breakfast-tray. That would give me the opportunity to disappear through the open door. But something made me hesitate. *I know him...*

Instead of avoiding him, I let him find me, his eyes widening as they met mine.

It was my old friend, Asher.

***

It had been many years since I had seen Asher, but one does not forget the face of a friend, especially when one has so few friends. I had startled him, but he relaxed when he saw my face. Obviously, he knew me as well.

"What are you doing here?" Then his eyes filled with dread, along with a deep, deep disappointment I will never forget. "Why are you dressed like that?"

"Close the door," I said. "It's better if we can talk undisturbed."

"You're a shadow-man, aren't you? It's the only way you could have gotten in here." Asher had always been a stoic, reluctant to let his feelings show. Still, his face paled a little. "Where is the Master?"

"Let's sit and talk for a moment. Obviously, you know about the shadow-men, a fact which doesn't surprise me, as you are an apprentice lore-master. That said, you should know that I have an assortment of blades concealed on my person, and I can kill you before you make another sound if I wish. Now close the door, will you? And lock it, too, while you're at it."

We sat down together, old friends reunited under the worst possible circumstances. Asher would hate me for what I had done to Martell, and I wanted to make him understand. I hoped I would not have to kill him. As usual, he came straight to the point.

"You killed the Master, didn't you?" I saw a bit of his old defiance in his eyes. "It's what you people do, isn't it…murder old men in their beds?"

"He killed himself, actually, but I would have done it had he not." I saw the grief in my former friend's eyes, and for the first time since I became a shadow-man, I felt doubt I could not dispel. Asher had always been trustworthy, and I had admired his intelligence. Now he was apprenticed to the Chief Lore-master, an honor reserved for the most exceptional student. What accolade had I earned? I was stealthy and had learned to kill people in various creative ways.

Asher started to rise. "I want to see him."

"I don't think that's wise, Asher. Not as yet. You can go back there once I'm gone." I felt my gaze harden as I asked the next question. "You're not going to make me kill you, are you?"

I saw a new emotion in my friend's face then, and he sat back down. "Unfortunately, I probably will. But you will tell me a few things first."

"Very well," I said. "But I can't stay long. What would you have me tell?"

"First, how did the Master die?"

"Moon-flower."

"Your moon-flower, I suppose?"

I shrugged. "He took it from my hand and drank it down. There was enough there to kill ten men, and he went quickly and peacefully."

Asher nodded. "He kept his dignity, then. I know how important that would have been to him. Did he say anything to you first?"

I looked away. This was a harder question to answer. Finally, I nodded.

"Did he speak of Darius, the madman?"

"He may have mentioned it." I looked at Asher's face, which was now filled with disgust. "Is it true?"

"Of course it is, although I'm sure whoever holds your leash has kept it from you. We mustn't have our trained killers questioning orders, after all."

His words stung my pride, and I grew angry. "No, we mustn't! I'm no different from a soldier who goes into battle…I defend the City, and I don't ask questions any more than the soldier who charges into the fray. I place those decisions in the hands of my superiors, and I follow orders."

"You really believe there's no difference between the battlefield and the bed-chamber? You chose this life, didn't you? I'm thinking you decided to quit asking questions because it made your life easier, especially after they flattered and praised you and gave you everything you wanted. I'm sure they made a particular point of convincing you of how valuable and special you are. Now you've killed the most enlightened man in the City because a madman told you to." He shook his head in disbelief and resignation. "Well, I'm going to see the Master. Then I suppose you should just kill me, because I don't want to live in a place where great and noble minds are snuffed out by what's left of King Darius." He looked me in the eye. "Think about it, Beltran. Have you ever even *seen* the King?"

Naturally, I hadn't. And, though I had honestly believed Darius to be wise and just, it was only because I had been told so. I had seen no real evidence of it. Still, I clung to that belief.

"If the King is such a dangerous madman, why does no one rise up against him? Surely those closest to him are aware…"

Asher looked at me as if I were the most unintelligent, gullible person ever to walk the world. "He's wealthy, powerful, and he has an incredibly vicious and formidable collection of personal guards. They won't let any harm come to him, and, because of killers like you, any attempt at reform or revolution cannot succeed." He paused for a moment. "And when's the last time you thought of your sister? I hope she remained ignorant of your chosen profession."

I felt as though a large stone lay in my gut. It had, indeed, been a long while since I had thought of Salina. I hadn't caught a glimpse of her anywhere...not the marketplace, not the temple, not the well...would I want her to know how I made my living? I heard her words in my ear...the words she had spoken when she was just a child. *You'll kill a lot of people someday, Glennroy.* She probably already knew.

Asher got up without asking my permission and started for Martell's bed-chamber.

I followed him, though I had no idea of what I would do...of how this would end. We stood beside the old man's peaceful form. Were it not for the fact that he wasn't breathing and his face had gone grayish-white, we would have thought he was sleeping.

Asher placed a gentle hand on his silvery hair. "I haven't seen his brow so smooth in years. I suppose his thoughts have quieted and his worries have gone." He turned to me. "It looks as if he's been tended to...someone closed his eyes, arranged the coverlet, and so on. Was that you?"

I nodded. "He seemed a kindly old fellow."

"Thanks for that. It means there's still hope for you, Beltran." We both heard stirrings in the corridor outside—the City was coming to life. "You had better kill me, unless your doubts have taken root and you're wondering whether a life spent serving King Darius is really what you thought it would be. I would ask only one other thing of you. Will you oblige me?"

"If I can."

"Go and find King Darius, and see him for yourself. Once you have seen him, you'll understand." He sat down in a chair beside his Master's bed. "Well, get on with it." He sighed. "I wish the Master hadn't taken all the moon-flower."

"Don't worry...I have more." I stood in silence for a moment, looking at the two scholars, one of whom had been my friend. I knew I should kill Asher—a shadow-man leaves no witnesses. I knew I could make it appear that he had died by his own hand, no doubt overcome with grief. But the doubts concerning Darius—the very purpose of my life—would not leave me. I might have been a shadow-man, but I was also Glennroy, son of Glenndon. Or was I? Had I become so willing to move at the bidding of another that I would murder a friend?

If you still believe what you have always been told, then kill him. If your doubts overrule your training, well, then leave him alive.

I knew there would be grave consequences if I failed to follow orders, but I also knew that I could not take another life until I had seen the truth of matters for myself. When I left the chamber, Asher was still very much alive.

***

First I went back to my own chambers. By the time I got there, I could hear the alarm-bells ringing in the Scholars' Keep. I smiled ruefully. Usually there would be competition among the remaining lore-masters, who would vie for Martell's position. Since it was fairly obvious that they, at least, were aware of who had ordered all the mysterious "natural deaths" of the King's enemies, I wondered whether they would now vie for the privilege of remaining in positions of lower rank.

Because my quarters were attached to the palace, I had a fair idea of who came and went and at what time. *I should go there tonight, after midnight, to be safe. But Darius will be sleeping then, surely...I want to see him in all his supposed madness.*

I changed into my regular garb, for I would go as Elmorah, not as Beltran the shadow-man. I wondered if anyone knew that I had spared Asher, who had promised not to tell anyone about me. While the scholars would know that Martell had been assassinated, they would not know by whose hand.

Still, I worried about my comrades-in-arms, Corvyn in particular. A shadow-man leaves no witnesses. Would they come after me for breaking the code?

I would go and seek Darius as soon as possible. The court would probably be in some uproar over the death of Martell...I would take advantage of the opportunity to observe the King during a difficult time. *Then again, he ordered Martell killed. This is probably not such a difficult time for him.*

It took me a while to find Darius—most of the day, in fact—and I can honestly say that my abilities had never been so sorely tested. Though I could walk freely in the common areas without raising so much as an eyebrow, the palace was filled with guards. Most of them looked formidable enough, and I certainly didn't want to attract any attention from them, but they would not lead me to the King. I would need to find the ones who guarded him. Known by their gold sashes, they were said to be the fiercest, most formidable, and most utterly humorless men in Orovar.

At last I knew I was getting close, as I observed a small company of gold-sashed men hulking down a corridor, their weapons clanking ominously. They made so much noise it was easy to follow behind them unnoticed...all I had to do was stay out of their torchlight. One bore a small metal casket, and I wondered what was inside, as the other men seemed to be distancing themselves from it. I followed them through a little-used part of the palace, down stairs and through corridors, until at last they moved into a dank chamber lit only by a few torches and the glow of a dying fire. I caught a whiff of the air that wafted toward me when the guards opened the heavy door. It smelled of sickness and decay.

This can't be where Darius is, I thought. *The King does not live in such a fetid hole, surely!* But the guards entered in single file, each one bowing and dropping briefly to one knee, and I knew I had to investigate. *If the King is there, and not a prisoner, then he must be mad!*

Perhaps that was it—the King had been imprisoned by his formidable guards, and that was why no one had seen him. And what would I do then?

One of the tools of my trade was a detailed map of the palace and all connected structures, as I often had to work my way into areas that were off limits to the rank and file—private bedchambers, prayer-rooms, and the like. I knew my way around already, but I had never been in this part of the palace before. The map showed the corridor and some interconnecting chambers at the end of it, all deep underground, but I knew I would never be able to get in through the door. *I don't need to get in. I just need to observe what's going on.* I remembered the fireplace, and I knew what I would do. There's always a gap between a stone chimney and a wooden ceiling. I consulted my map, preparing to make my way up to the next level.

A short while later I crouched beside the wide stone chimney that loomed up from the King's great fireplace, peering down through the space I knew would be there. I was glad of the chimney, as I would have to keep still and the damp air held a chill that made me shiver. The air didn't smell as bad from up here, either, but I could still detect the gut-churning scent of rotting flesh.

I could see a good bit of the room through the gap, which I had accessed from beneath the wooden floor of the level above. I knew it because underground chimneys were directed into smoke-holes that fed out into several massive stacks…we used to hang meat and fish in them, to great effect. But there was no meat or fish hung in the smoke from *this* fire.

The metal casket had been placed upon a small pedestal near a heavily-carved and richly upholstered chair. Both the chair and the pedestal stood upon a raised dais near the fireplace, and I had an excellent view of them. The guards sat or stood in various locations around the chamber. They did not speak, they hardly moved, and their faces were as stony as any I'd seen. I knew I would have no chance against them.

At last, a rustling and dragging sound came from an adjoining chamber, together with a harsh cackle that lifted the hair on the back of my neck. A wizened figure shuffled ungracefully into the room. The dragging left foot and withered left arm told the story—this man, if it was a man, had suffered an affliction of the brain. I saw the guards drop to one knee and bow their heads, and I saw the golden crown through the grayish-brown straw of the man's hair.

"Oh, get up, you fools. Have you brought me what I desire?" The voice was like metal scraping on roughened glass, and it sent a chill through me that I won't soon forget. Come to think of it, I will probably remember everything I saw, heard, and smelled there until the end of

The Shadow-Man

my days.

The figure shuffled to the dais and placed a pale, claw-like right hand on the lid of the casket in a fond caress. "Excellent. My pain has been very bad lately, Brodda, and the sparrows—they just won't stop screaming and chattering! Can you hear them?"

One of the guards bowed again. "Yes, My King."

"Then why can't you make them *stop*?"

Brodda thought for a moment. "There are too many, My King. But we have brought something to help you."

Darius lurched onto the dais and sat carefully down on his throne, obviously in pain. "Ahhh, yes. Your reward will be great, my friends and protectors. You have brought my enemy to me, and I will now feed off the treachery in his black heart." He turned his face upward for a moment, and I saw the ravages of disease there—the scars, the flesh eaten away, his nose a ghastly breathing-hole, the muscles of his jaw visible through the skin of his cheek. *He has been marked...marked by the Sickness. It has made him mad, like the others, only he's worse...much worse!*

To my horror, the King reached up with long, ragged fingernails and raked his own flesh with them, bringing a trickle of red. "With my blood, I vanquish that of my enemies, and all who would oppose us!" As the guards cheered, the one named Brodda stepped forward and lifted the lid of the casket. Darius reached inside with his now-bloody right hand and extracted a lump of dark red meat, still dripping.

"It's *cold*," whined the King. "You know how much I like to feel the heat of my foes, Brodda!" His lips drew back in a snarl, exposing a blackened mouth with several missing teeth. A coated, pale tongue darted quickly through the gaps, reminding me of a lizard.

Brodda took a step back, holding both hands up in

submission. "My King, you were resting, and left orders that we should not disturb you. Please forgive my incompetence. I will know better the next time."

"Yes, you will, I'm sure," said the King through his unspeakable mouth. "You will if you wish to keep on receiving the honors and accolades I give."

And if he wants to go on breathing, I thought.

"Heaven pound those damnable *sparrows!*" Darius jerked his head sideways and squeezed his eyes shut as though protecting them from imaginary birds whizzing about. A moment later he peered at the lump of meat like a bird of prey trying to decide which bits to tear into first. Then he brought the whole thing to his mouth and bit, ripping off nearly half of it before swallowing it whole. He licked the blood from the remainder before allowing it to fall from his fingers, staining his lap. Then he placed each gnarled finger in his mouth and sucked on it with a dreamy expression.

"The birds…the demon-birds are going…they're finally…quiet. Ahhhhhh. The pain…it's going away now. The pain is dying with the traitor's heart." He looked around at the guards, all of whom stared back at him in silence. "You have done well, and you will be rewarded…all of you." With that, he sank back, head lolling over, eyes still open but peaceful, as his bloody mouth kept whispering words I could not hear.

I had seen more than enough. This creature was Darius the Just? This was the man whose bidding I had followed, whose orders I had carried out? For how long had he been a madman? How many of those people were innocent? *This is the Moon Man, only much worse*, I thought. *This is the Moon Man with power—with an army of creatures who don't care what he asks of them as long as they are rewarded. Kind of like me.*

My revulsion and horror gave way to indignation. How

could this have gone on so long? Could I kill the wretch? He had to have been noble once. I know he had been. *It's wrong to leave him alive to suffer the ravages of his body and mind...*

At that moment, I felt a wrathful hand on my shoulder, and I knew I would have troubles of my own to worry about.

I turned my head, despite the hard, cold bite of the blade that was now held against my throat, and looked into the eyes of Corvyn, my Master.

***

Corvyn had done me the courtesy of escorting me back to my chambers. Now, surely, he would cut my throat. As usual, he came straight to the point. "Well, now you've done it. And you had such promise, too." He sighed. "At this rate, I'll never be able to retire."

"What in all the seven hells was that?" I said. "How can you serve that...that diseased, half-rotten carcass with the mind of a demon? He's not even human anymore."

"Oh, yes, he is," said Corvyn. "And he has his moments. You saw him on an average day...neither good nor bad. He still has better days."

I wondered what a bad day was like. "What was that thing he ate? He said it was like the traitor's heart. What was it?"

Corvyn sighed, and he spoke to me in a tone I hadn't heard since I was a young apprentice. "It was Martell's heart, or part of it, anyway. What did you think it was?"

"But...why?" I asked, trying hard to imagine what would drive a man to literally eat another man's heart.

"He's mad, you idiot. It does no good to ask why. He thinks it gives him power, and he knows it takes his pain away. Think about it—Martell's blood would have been full of moon-flower. Just enough to send Darius into whatever pleasant imaginings he still holds dear."

"And you...you serve him willingly? How can you?" I asked.

"Because I like life, and I want to keep living it," said Corvyn. "If I didn't kill the King's enemies, someone else would, believe me. And, when Darius falls, we'll most likely both be out of work. I'm too good at what I do. Besides, I'm too old to start over in a different trade."

"Well, I'm *not*."

"That's true, Beltran, you're not. But there is no leaving our profession any way other than feet first. I'm sure you know that. You're a shadow-man—the King's man—until he says you're not. Then you're no one's man at all."

"I didn't sign on for this," I said, the blood rising in my face. "How many of those people—the ones we were sent to kill—were innocent?"

Corvyn shrugged, examining the nails of his right hand. I knew he would kill me in a heartbeat if I made any sort of hostile move. "I've no idea, but I would say none of them were innocent. They threatened the King, and we took care of business. That's all I need to know." He looked up at me then, his eyes glittering with cold humor. "You knew this job was dangerous when you took it. You agreed not to make judgments, but to do what you were told, and your life has been easy and pleasurable. Up to now, you've done very well." He sighed. "I'm sorry you ran into your friend at Martell's. I'm disappointed you left him alive. Now I'm afraid I have few choices with respect to you."

My hands were shaking, for I knew I had come to the end of my life. Corvyn was still twice the assassin I was, and he was fully armed. I, of course, was not. "Well, at least tell me this—how long has Darius been mad? He wasn't always that way, was he?"

"I've always tried to be honest with you, at least as far as my position would allow," said Corvyn. "If it makes you feel any better, Darius used to be a great man. He ruled this City wisely and well for a long time, but he was always reclusive. Therefore, when he got the Sickness, no one knew about it other than his personal physician and his most trusted ministers. He recovered, but the plague left its mark on him. I see in your eyes that you understand."

"Still, I have seen many who were marked by the Sickness, but almost never this bad, and they didn't live long. There has to be something else at work."

"They probably didn't have personal physicians or a whole arsenal of medicinals to aid them," said Corvyn. "Still, you're right. There is something else. Darius found himself in bed with the wrong consort. I will say no more."

I knew there were blights that passed from person to person in the bed-chamber, and I had taken careful steps to avoid them, but apparently Darius had not been careful enough. "That explains some of it," I said. "But, if he was a noble man, and you cared for him, how can you let him suffer as he is? He was your King, and yet you all leave him to linger in pain and depravity?"

Corvyn, to my disappointment, rolled his eyes heavenward. "Did I ever say I *cared* for him? I'm not as sentimental as you are. His troubles are of his own making, and his ministers have been managing the City's affairs for years, anyway. If he had taken better care, he would have been fine. Besides, I'm just a lowly minion. A shadow-man doesn't ask questions, remember? You might care for him, but the person you should be most concerned about, in this moment, is yourself."

I swallowed hard, trying not to let my terror be heard. "Will you at least grant me a painless end, then?"

Corvyn's eyes flashed. "You would give up so easily? Let me truly answer your question with another question. Why did you not kill Darius yourself?"

"I...I didn't have time. I was actually thinking about it when you grabbed my shoulder."

"You had plenty of time. If I turned you loose right now, would you just go and kill him, then?"

"I...I don't know..."

"No, you wouldn't, because it would mean your certain death, and you know it. You're not ready to die, and neither am I. Neither of us has the fortitude to put Darius out of his misery—we're still enjoying life too much. Isn't that so?"

"I hate you, did you know it? I really hate you," I said.

"You hate me because I'm always right. Still, I'm not going to kill you. Not today."

I stood in silence for a moment.

"What, nothing to say? I should have thought some thanks would be in order. Or don't you trust me to keep my word?"

"No...I do trust you where your word is concerned. You might have kept the truth from me, but you never actually lied to me. Not when you made a point of having given your word."

He smiled a little. "Well, then, let me tell you how it's going to be. I was ordered to kill you already, and I will if I catch you again. As I said, you should not have left your friend alive."

"How did you know about that?"

"Don't interrupt! I'll give you a seven-hour head start. Pack your gear and leave the City. You should go north and west, into the desert."

"The desert? Alone? But that's madness! Besides, you'll be looking for me!"

"Not there, I won't, and no one will blame me. A man would have to be a lot stupider than you are to flee into that wasteland, right?" He paused for a moment, as though lost in a memory. "You came from desert lands, didn't you?"

"As a boy. We lived at the edge of the Stone Desert," I said. "But it's been years since…"

"Well, you'd better pack plenty of water then, hadn't you? And you'll need to remember every bit of desert lore you might once have been gifted with. No one will follow you there, because they know you're smarter than that, but that's the way you'll have to go. I'll still be looking for you, and if you choose not to take my advice, and go along the civilized trade routes through gentler lands, I'll find you. If I do, Darius will eat your heart."

He looked hard at me for another long moment. "I'm giving you a chance, though even I don't really understand why. I guess I just hate to see all my hard efforts utterly wasted."

I closed my eyes and bowed my head. "Thank you, Master."

When I looked up again, he placed a clever hand on my shoulder. "You have seven hours from this moment. If it is meant that you should live, you will."

***

I packed as much water as I could carry, along with my weapons, food, and other necessities. I included two phials of Moon-flower, on Corvyn's advice. "Dying of thirst is terrible," he said. "You will face many terrible deaths where you're going. This will give you the release you need, should fortune abandon you."

I left the tools of the assassin's trade behind—wires, cord, elixirs, mask—as I expected my days of murdering people by stealth and poison were now behind me. Then, at the last moment, I retrieved the mask I had used to smother my victims, and examined the underside of it closely. Here, etched in the soft leather, were the stains of sweat, saliva, and tears from people who, I now knew, probably had not deserved to die. I could smell the faint aroma of their last moments. Here was a small spot of dried blood. Here was a bite-mark from a man who had struggled a little too hard. The stains looked up at me, accusing me, and I knew I would have to keep the wretched thing with me as a reminder of what I had done. My hands trembled as I tucked it away in my pack.

Seven hours.

I wished I had the time to find my sister and say goodbye, but I didn't even know where she was. As a favored King's Man I had been given a fine horse, but he was recovering from a foreleg strain and I knew he wouldn't get far. I thought about stealing a horse, but there would be little to feed or water it with once I gained the desert. Besides that, Corvyn had given me seven hours of grace, but the owner of the stolen horse might not. It's easier to track a horse than a man.

It was still daylight when I left Orovar, heading out to the north and west, toward the desert. As I passed unseen beyond the City walls, I heard a flock of sparrows chattering and fussing in a thorn-thicket. Their chittering, strident calls were actually quite irritating. *So, this is what he hears all day and night*, I thought, and shook my head in sympathy.

I remember relatively little of the desert crossing, at least after about the first fortnight. I did all right by myself for a while, rationing food and water carefully, relying on the signs to find what little water could be had. I was amazed at how much of it I remembered. But the farther I drew from Orovar, the more difficult things became. I walked all night and rested all day in whatever shade I could manage, grateful that I had not been sent out in midsummer.

Regrettably, I drank some bad water I had found, and it sickened me. I knew better, but I was just so *thirsty*, and for a while it seemed I would suffer little in the way of consequences. But then came the griping of the bowels and the cramping in my stomach. I lost all the water I had consumed, plus a whole lot more. I lay in the shade of stones, moaning and weeping, shivering as if with cold, knowing I would soon die. Still, I could not bring myself to take the moon-flower...not yet.

I remember lying on my back, looking up at the stars. No other sky can rival the velvety black of a desert night, spangled with so many brilliant gems that, even after all this time, it takes my breath away. I was so thirsty, and my insides were burning, and I was dying. *I should take the moon-flower*, I thought. Yes, just take it and drift away among those innumerable stars. Trembling, I reached for my pack. As my hand closed around it, I jerked back, startled by the pair of booted feet that had appeared only inches away. It was Asher, though my vision was so uncertain that I couldn't see him clearly.

"How...how did you find me?" I croaked, for I had not used my voice, except to weep and moan, for many days. "Do you have water?"

Asher's normally stoic face broke into a warm smile. "No, I'm afraid I don't have any water. Finding you wasn't difficult. You left plenty of tracks. Now, let's get on your feet. You don't yet know it, but there's a tavern not far away on the other side of these rocks."

"A tavern? Out here? You're mad," I muttered.

"Am I? Get up and see for yourself."

I struggled to my feet and staggered around the pile of stones, following behind Asher, who was full of energy and nearly left me behind.

"Wait!" I cried, nearly falling to my knees again.

"Don't worry, I won't leave you. Just look there!" He pointed to what could only be a tavern, and I wanted to weep at the sight of it. The legend on the sign was written in a tongue I did not understand, but the old, weathered wood bore the image of a seven-pointed star. *Thank the powers of heaven, for they are sure to have water,* I thought, but Asher stopped me at the door.

"People may come here, and people may go. You should not speak to anyone who does not speak to you first, understand?"

"Fine," I said. "Just get me inside so I can have a little water, and I'll do whatever you ask."

When I first entered the tavern, I saw only a few people inside. I couldn't see any of their faces, as they wore their hoods drawn over them, but that wasn't unusual in a place like this. Asher led me to a scarred wooden table, and I sat down heavily in one of the chairs. "Someone bring me some water, please," I muttered. It had taken most of my strength to make the trek, and I could feel an ominous cramping in my nether regions again. "Water will make everything right, won't it, Asher?" I looked at his face in the candle-light. "You look really pale, my friend. I'm thinking you could use a good, long drink yourself."

"Water won't help me," said Asher. "But don't worry…you'll find it soon. First, we must talk." He reached up and unwrapped the dusty brown scarf from around his neck, revealing the gaping red wound in his throat. I could hear air whistling through it whenever he spoke. I was rendered speechless for a moment, trying to fathom what had happened, when he saved me the trouble.

"Corvyn, your Master, came to see me after you left Martell," he said simply. "I'll have to admit, the man is good. I never heard him coming, and I only saw his face because he allowed me to. Apparently, you should have killed me. He was just finishing your job for you." He wrapped the scarf back around his neck, hiding the wound, to my relief. "You should know that everyone is accusing you of two murders now."

"Then...you're dead," I said dully.

Asher laughed, and the scarf couldn't mask the wheezing coming from his slashed throat. "Your ability to solve mysteries has improved, Beltran. But since you spared my life, I am pleased to return the favor. You will not die this night. First, you must face your guilt."

The tavern was now filled with people, and I could hear them muttering. Some of those mutterings were none too friendly. "Who are they?" I asked, shrinking back in my chair a little.

"You're an intelligent man. You'll figure it out," said Asher, and for the first time I didn't care for the smile he wore. "Remember to speak only when you are spoken to."

Several men were seated at one large table near the wall, and they lowered their hoods, turning to face me. I didn't recognize any of them...not at first. They scowled at me.

"He doesn't even know who we are—any of us," said one.

"Give him a moment," said the man on his left. "He'll remember." He held up his right hand, showing a golden ring with a great, red stone that glittered even in the dim light.

I remembered him now. He was one of the first men I killed.

A light kindled in his eyes. "Ah. You see? I knew he wouldn't forget my ring, anyway. Well, Shadow-man, do you recall our faces now?"

"He spoke to me, right? I can answer him, can't I?" I whispered to Asher, who smiled and nodded. "Yes, I remember you," I said. "Although...I cannot seem to place the man sitting nearest the wall." The man I referred to looked at me with pure, unabashed hatred. For the life of me, I could not recall him.

"I'm one of the ones who actually had plotted against King Darius," said the man with the ring. My name was Rubio, remember? I'm one of the few who actually might have deserved your attentions! Ha!"

"Who is that man near the wall?" I asked, feeling a cold chill take hold in the pit of my stomach.

Rubio looked over at his companions. "Oh, him? That's Vero. You don't recognize him because it was so dark in the bed-chamber. Thing is, you killed him by mistake! He wasn't supposed to be there. That's why he hates you so much. If I were you, I wouldn't speak to him at all, even if he speaks to you."

Rubio's cold, reptilian eyes glinted in the candle-light. "You're in a dangerous place here, Shadow-man."

I turned to Asher. "What is the purpose of this? Are these people...are they all people whose lives I ended? Have they come to torment me? I thought you were my friend. Why have you brought me here?" I felt my eyes widen as I realized something else, to my horror. "There isn't any water, is there?"

Asher held up his hand. "Save your strength. You must hear them out—all of them. They have things to say."

I don't know how much time passed. I don't remember

how many souls I heard that night...I lost count after a while. A few knew why their deaths had been ordered, but most did not. They wanted me to tell them. In a few instances, I could relate what I had been told, but it didn't help them. They would shriek and rail and scream that it wasn't true—that they had been killed for no reason. Then they would vanish in a whirl of smoke and light and tears.

Finally, Vero rose and approached my table. He raised his hand as if to strike me, but seemed to remember it would do not good. When he spoke, his voice was like a razor cutting into my flesh. "You've ended my life, Shadow-man, and I would curse you if I could. But I was a good man in life, and I will continue to be a good man now. I would not wish your guilt or your wretchedness on anyone." He turned to leave, grabbing his tankard in one massive hand. Then, at the last, he turned back to me, draining the tankard in several long, satisfying swallows. I nearly wept with desire for just one drink, and he smirked at me. "Sorry...somehow I just can't bring myself to share," he said, then walked into the mist, clapping his fellows on the back and laughing.

"You're lucky that's all he did to you," said Asher in a solemn voice. "But he held on to his humanity—to the things his father taught him. Didn't your father teach you that it's wrong to kill?"

"Yes," I said, so exhausted I didn't know if I could draw another breath. "When does this end? Can't I just die in peace?"

"Not quite yet. One more soul would speak with you this night." He beckoned to a lone figure still seated in a misty corner. "He's ready for you now, I think. Come on. He won't stand much more."

The figure moved to sit beside me, reaching out with one pale hand...a hand with ragged nails and fingers marred and torn as though they had been chewed. *Salina!*

She lowered her hood, and I could see the terrible bruises on her face. One eye was swollen shut, but the other glowed with warmth and love for me. "What happened?" I muttered, tears coming despite how dry I was.

"Someone didn't like the dreams Salina had concerning him," said Asher. "He beat her to death years ago." He shook his head. "You didn't even know, did you?"

"I'm in a good place now," said Salina. "I can't tell you any more than that, as it is forbidden. But you have things to do with your life still, Glennroy. You have to bring yourself out of darkness. You were brave once, brave and good, but you have spent your life in the shadows, hiding from your victims, hiding from yourself. You went too far."

I couldn't speak. I didn't know what to say. I wanted to tell her how much I loved her, how sorry I was that I had thought only of myself all these years, but I just couldn't find the words.

"Shhh. Don't cry, Glennroy," she said. "I know what's in your heart. You don't have to say it." She smiled—the bright, hopeful smile I had known when she was a child. "You have to survive, and find yourself again. There is much good that you may do, and you must atone for the evil you have done. Only know that I love you, and I forgave you long ago. Your destiny wasn't really yours to control until now. You have been given another chance. Use it well."

By the time I managed to choke out the words "Don't leave me," she was gone.

I turned on Asher. "Why did you bring me here? How can I ever atone for so many? I was only doing what I was told to do, in the King's service! This isn't my fault. And I need *water!*"

I leaped up from the table and lunged over to the long oaken bar, where the tavern-keeper stood, regarding me with a placid expression. "Are you deaf?" I yelled. "I need water!" I reached across the bar, enraged, and grabbed the man by the front of his shirt. I could hear Asher laughing behind me, but I was intent on the tavern-keeper and would not release him. "Water," I shouted again, "or you will regret it!"

To my horror, the tavern-keeper's face began to change. His nose elongated and his chin shrank, his eyes moved around to the sides of his head, the pupils transforming into horizontal black bars as the color lightened from brown to amber. Coarse, thick hair began to appear, covering his face and sprouting out of his shirt collar, as two dreadful-looking horns emerged from the top his head. He opened his now-tiny mouth and let forth a long, piercing bleat.

"Ba-a-a-a-a-a-a-a-a-a-aaaa!"

The tavern-keeper had turned into a goat before my eyes. I had never before heard a goat laugh, but I was hearing one now. And Asher, who was still there for a moment longer, laughed with him. "You still have a long way to go, my friend. You have to accept your guilt and learn to live with it. Then, maybe, you can be free. Goodbye…and good luck!"

Darkness overtook me and I fell to the floor, hearing only the voice of the wretched goat-man in my ears.

***

I heard the voice of the goat again, only this time I could also hear the sound of a copper bell. I imagined I could smell the goat, too. *How wonderful—odor of ghostly goat.*

When I felt something touching my shoulder, I cried out, terrified. The goat-man would surely get me! Then the sun hit my face, and I knew I was no longer in the tavern. Beings like the goat-man would never come out in the sun.

I moaned piteously and opened my eyes. A goat-face loomed directly over me, licking and chewing as goats will, but it was a real goat. *And with goats...come goat-herds...* I felt my spirit leap as hope seized it, struggling to turn away from the rock and toward the open air. Here were men...herdsmen...and a caravan! I tried to cry out, my throat was too dry and raw to make a sound.

Help me. Oh, please help me! Then darkness again.

When I came to the second time, a woman was holding a water-skin to my lips. "Careful," she said in heavily-accented Aridani. "Only one swallow."

I knew better than to drink too much water at once, but it was so hard not to. Still, I disciplined myself, taking one swallow at a time, pausing for what seemed an eternity, and then another swallow. I was given a small piece of salted meat, already obligingly chewed for me. The salt tasted wonderful and made me feel even better.

I had been saved, but for what purpose I did not yet know.

***

A long-established desert custom holds that when you find a man dying of thirst, you give him water even if the man is an enemy. Sharing your water guarantees that, should you find yourself in a similar state, anyone who finds you will share his. "The Wheel turns," as the desert people say.

The people of the caravan took me in, and they were

courteous enough, but no more than required. I did my best to repay them, though I knew I could never make up for what I owed. I told them my name was El-morah, and I tried to make myself useful, but they kept me at a distance, as though they didn't trust me. In fact, my only friends were the goats. They followed me everywhere, to my dismay. I knew I owed my life to them, but since my encounter with the goat-man I have viewed them with a suspicious eye.

One day I noticed one of the men struggling to lift a heavy bundle onto the back of one of the dromadin, and I moved to aid him. He wasn't in a position to prevent me, but he shot me a look that clearly said I was unwelcome. "You will please stay away from the dromadin, and from our provisions," he said.

I should have simply bowed and backed away, but I didn't. "Why? I am no thief. Do you believe I would harm you?"

"Not a thief? Of *course* you aren't," he said. "I've never met a thief yet who would not deny it." He looked hard into my eyes. "The only reason a man would be this far out in the desert alone is if someone drove him there. Only criminals are driven into the wastes alone, and only a madman would go there of his own accord. So, which are you—criminal or madman?"

I didn't know what to say. "Well, I'm not a madman…"

"Then why were you driven here? No…never mind. I don't want to know. Just stay away from our provisions in the future." With that, he turned and left me standing alone, my face burning with shame. What would I have told him had he let me answer?

Am I a criminal? I was driven from the City, but not for what I had done. I have a price on my head for what I did not do. And who was really to blame? I drew a deep sigh and went back to the goats. At least they didn't pass judgment on me. After I thought on it for a while, I decided it was Corvyn's fault. He was the one who kept secrets...he told me all those tales about how those people deserved to die. If not for Corvyn, my life would have been very different.

As Asher would have observed, I still had a long way to go.

The first glimmer of light came in the form of a young woman named Fythia. She, like me, was an outcast, a Plague survivor with no other family, and she had paid for the privilege of traveling with the caravan. Since she had paid, she did no other work, and therefore had little to occupy her time. In fact the others in the caravan shunned her, and she no doubt longed for human company. I know I did.

I had filled back out nicely, and many would consider me handsome—I've been told I have a pleasantly rugged face and fine, strong shoulders. I caught her casting appreciative glances my way—I was no stranger to female attention, after all—and resolved to try and talk with her. It wouldn't be that difficult, as she was always alone.

When I approached her she seemed almost fearful, and would not look directly at me, let alone speak. I caught the disapproving looks and sneering faces of others in the caravan, and thought I had guessed what the trouble might be.

On one rather chilly night, I found her trying to start a small fire. She struck her flint again and again, but raised only an occasional tiny spark.

"You need a new flint."

I had come quietly up from behind, and I startled her, though I hadn't meant to. She drew back from me, one arm held up, protecting her face. *Who has hurt you so badly?* I knelt down, drew forth my own flint-and-steel, and quickly got the fire smoldering. A bit of careful fanning brought it into flame.

I handed her my flint. "Here you are. You should have no more trouble, and I have another one. May I share your fire for a while?"

She nodded, and spoke to me for the first time. "Since you kindled it, it is yours to share."

After that, we talked often. I never pressed her, and I tried not to ask difficult questions. She returned the favor, and we spent many pleasant hours wandering among the goats.

The caravan made its way between oases, traveling by night and resting by day, and I discovered that Fythia shared my fascination with the stars.

Finally, one night, I decided to see what I could find out about her. I had my suspicions, and I hoped to learn the truth. "Do you know where the caravan is going? No one seems to want to tell me," I said.

She looked hard at me. "Does it matter?"

"Well, no…not really, but I am curious. Where are we going?"

"We are going to a place called the Sandstone. I have been there…hopefully you'll find what you need."

"Why are you going there?"

"Because I need to go somewhere, don't I? With luck, I'll be able to earn a meager living there."

"I have heard the men of the caravan say that you have no family." I felt a small lump in my throat. "That must be hard."

"Well, you would know, wouldn't you? I see it in your eyes," she said. "It seems we have both been driven out of the lands we knew, away from people we loved. I know why I can't go back. Why can't you?"

"I have a price on my head," I said simply. "But I am

not guilty of the crime I was charged with."

"No, none of you is *ever* guilty," she said. "I, on the other hand, am entirely to blame for my own predicament." She looked into my eyes then, her gaze as old as shame itself. "You might not want to sit beside me."

I knew then that my suspicions had been correct. "You were a hired consort, am I right?"

"I was...until I fell in with the wrong master. I'll never lie with a man again."

"You did it to survive, didn't you? The Plague took your family, even as it took most of mine. We had to get along however we could."

She smiled, but there was no humor in it. "I chose my path, El-morah."

"What was your other choice? Starving to death?"

Her mouth drew into a thin, hard line. "Compared with some fates, starving to death doesn't seem so bad."

I looked at the dark red blotch on the back of her left wrist. No wonder she tried to keep it covered. She had fallen in with the wrong master, all right.

"I know you have the Blight," I said. "Don't worry...I won't say anything to anyone. I swear it on my life."

The color drained from her face, and she looked away. A moment later, I heard her weeping. "If you want to share a different fire, I understand. Aren't you afraid of me now? Everyone else is. The last settlement I tried to call home thought they would burn me alive to cure me." She shook her head. "Not that I blame them..."

"Blight isn't passed by sitting near the same fire," I said. "And no, I'm not afraid of you. How did you escape?"

"Someone realized that burning a sick woman to death is wrong, and wasn't afraid to act on it," she said. "I hope he wasn't punished too severely. Now, since you are still willing to speak with me, what's your story? What crime are you innocent of?"

"Do you really want to hear my story?" I asked.

"More than anything. It will take my thoughts from my own troubles, and maybe it will even help you with yours."

I knew she would keep my secrets—she had no one to tell them to, anyway. It took several nightly campfires to do it, but I told her everything. To her credit, she didn't appear to be shocked or to think any less of me, and that bolstered my confidence. When I finally finished, she sat silent for a moment. Then, tenderly, she took my hand.

"There is something...something difficult I need to ask you," she said. "I want to ask a favor, though I know I have not earned that right. Still, we are friends, yes?"

"How could you doubt it? I have just bared my soul to you. I have trusted you with all my secrets," I said.

"Then hear me, El-morah, who was once called Beltran the Shadow-man. You know I have the Blight. We both know what it does to people."

I recalled the ravings of King Darius. "Yes. I have seen what it can do."

"If madness tries to take me, I would ask your assistance in ending my pain," she said. "I want to die fully aware, as myself, not as a madwoman. Please, will you promise me?"

I didn't know what to say for a moment. If taking life is wrong, and I had been wrong for doing it...but was it *always* wrong?

"All I'm asking is to end my life with the same dignity granted to a dog or a hopelessly lame horse," she said, tears welling in her eyes. "You have the knowledge and the will to take life without causing pain. Will you not help a friend?"

She would not end up like Darius if I could help it.

"When the time comes, I will," I said. "I promise."

Often, as I lay in whatever shade I could find during the day, I reflected on the things she had told me. *She chose her path, as I chose mine, but she has been willing to bear the consequences, whereas I have not. She has twice my fortitude.*

Even so, I was still blaming others for my situation—Corvyn, Darius, even Asher. He should never have taken me to the tavern. No man could withstand such an assault—being overwhelmed by all those angry souls. No wonder I was in such conflict. And I did want to atone—I *did!* I just couldn't begin to know how to do it.

I hoped for another visit from Salina, or even Asher. Perhaps they could guide me. But the only visits I had were those I didn't want. I had the worst nightmares of my life, usually involving my smothering-mask. I would be sitting alone under the moon, gazing at it, when the faces would appear there, struggling for breath. I heard their voices—*you did this to me! You took me from my wife and children! You didn't even know me!*—and I would try to appease them.

I know…I'm sorry. I did what I was hired to do. I'm sorry! I had no choice. I'm sorry…

I would awaken in a cold sweat, trembling all over. Once I yelled so loud that Fythia heard me. She was there, wiping the sweat from my forehead, when I came to myself. "You kept saying 'I'm sorry.' But, in my experience, the man who has to keep saying so isn't sorry enough yet. Guilt has a terrible hold on you—the only way to be free is to accept it."

"I've heard that before," I said, as my heart slowed to normal and I stopped trembling. "It seems I don't know how to do that."

"It's not as hard as it seems," she said with a gentle,

genuine smile. "You just have to stop making excuses. You will have to admit to being what you are…and then start again."

***

The leader of the caravan, a tall, bearded man named Mathis, summoned everyone to the evening fire as we approached the western boundary of the Stone Desert. It wouldn't be that much longer until we would arrive at the Sandstone, and the closer one gets to civilized lands, the greater the likelihood of trouble.

"I have called you together because the lands we are about to travel through are perilous," he said. "Word has spread of a gang of bandits who roam here, and they show no mercy to travelers. They don't merely take valuables—they take lives, and I will need every man willing to fight. If you have weapons, hone them. If you do not, see me and I will make sure you are well armed. That's all I have to say."

Plague had swept through these lands nearly thirty years ago, and lawlessness had been on the rise ever since. They were times of relative plenty, because the number of people had been slashed, and there were far more resources to go around. But those who did not want to earn their wealth by honest means had taken to a darker, easier road, and they would take whatever they found from anyone they could.

Mathis came to see me after the others had dispersed. It was the first time we had spoken. "Well, El-morah, we are bound to run into bad people here. The question is, where do your loyalties lie?"

I stared at him. "What do you mean?"

"Your reputation is none too savory. You consort with that woman, and the circumstances in which we found you are suspicious at best. You have never really given us a satisfactory explanation."

"No one has asked me for one," I said, feeling my hackles rising. "Do you now regret your hospitality? I am grateful and indebted to you for saving my life, and I will fight to defend you should need arise, but if you would feel better about it, give me a few provisions and I will try to make the rest of the journey on my own."

"That would mean sentencing you to death," said Mathis. "We are not prepared to do that...not yet. And you're right. If bandits should attack us, we'll need every available man." He turned to leave, bowing his head briefly in a curt gesture of farewell. I bowed in return.

"The Wheel turns," I said. "I will do what I can to aid you."

"Yes," said Mathis. "The Wheel turns."

I had never been in an actual battle before. I had trained as a soldier and had become skilled with various weapons, but apart from quelling minor civil unrest, that was as far as I had gotten before Corvyn took me under his wing. We were not entirely unprepared, as we had heard one of the bandits' horses calling to one of our own, but we didn't have much time to brace for the attack. They came pouring out of the hills just to the north of the road—nearly a hundred of them—and I knew the Wheel would not be turning in our favor that night. We should have known better than to travel under the full moon.

We were easy targets, though the men fought hard to protect their brothers and sons. Only two women traveled with us—Fythia and an older woman named Kashma, who, I had learned, was Mathis's sister. She had been the first to give me water. I never knew what happened to her.

I killed a lot of men that night, casting whatever blades

I could find at any rider who passed. I'm agile and I know how to stay out of the way. I say with some pride that if there had been ten more of me, things might have gone differently. But the men of the caravan relied on swords, which cannot be hurled and require close contact with an enemy. When that enemy is mounted on a swift horse in the dark, a swordsman has little chance.

We had a few archers of worth, but they had more, and only a few of our folk were mounted. Those who stood on their own feet were soon peppered with arrows from the short, stout horse-bows of the mounted bandits. The Wheel was turning, all right, and I knew the caravan had no chance.

I called out to Fythia, but did not see her. *Perhaps she has fled to the hills...made her escape...I could do that, too. I certainly know how to disappear. The battle is hopeless, and whether I stay or go will make no difference in the end.*

But I realized something about myself in that moment—that I am a man of courage. I could not abandon these innocents to their fate, though I did not know them. I would atone for some of the sorrow and death I had wrought. I defended them, even though they held no love for me. I took arrows for them—one in my shoulder and one in my right thigh—though they had not trusted me. I would prove myself now, and I didn't care what happened.

I could almost hear Corvyn's voice, laughing and calling me a fool, but I didn't care. *I am responsible for my own destiny! No one else—only me.* I fought now for something greater than myself, and it felt good.

I battled like a lion until one of the wounded dromadin crashed down on top of me, driving the arrow deeper into my thigh, forcing the breath from my body, and causing unspeakable pain. I ground my teeth together so hard that

I felt one crack, just before blessed darkness took me.

I don't know how long I lay trapped beneath the dead dromadin before my senses returned—I knew only that the sun had risen. The pain was simply exquisite, radiating from arrow wounds and broken bones. I could tell several of my ribs were cracked, and I could barely breathe for the weight of the beast. A wave of nausea flooded through my innards and I fought it back, knowing that if I tried to vomit, I would die.

I couldn't move, and I had no water. I was finished.

"You understand now, don't you?" said a soft voice. I tried to turn my head, but I couldn't see who had spoken.

"Fythia? Fythia, is that you? Come here, where I can see you."

"I'm afraid I can't," she said. "I'm dying, you see, and I haven't the strength to move. But I can at least die in my right mind, beside my friend."

"I'm sorry," I said. "I hoped you had gone to the hills...that you had escaped."

"Escaped to what? Dying alone in the desert, or raving mad with Blight? My life was over a long time ago. Yours, though, is just beginning."

"You might be wrong about that, I'm afraid," I said. "I'll be lucky to see another moon-rise."

"It's all right. You understand now. You chose to die defending the caravan, though the people did not love you. You chose to save their lives, even as you chose to take life before."

"Yes, I chose," I said. "And there is no one else to blame." These words were very hard for me to say, and I thought I was going to weep. I felt hollow inside. "I am what my choices have made me—it has always been so."

"So it is with all of us."

She drew a deep, sighing breath, and I knew I wouldn't

have her company for much longer. I waited, hoping she would speak again.

"El-morah, have you accepted your guilt? It seems you have."

Tears welled in my eyes—tears of pain, regret, and relief. "Yes. Yes I have, though it burns my soul. How does anyone bear it?"

"It just takes time. You'll see." She was silent for a moment. "It's been a long time since anyone loved you, hasn't it?"

I thought for a moment. The only person who had truly loved me in the last thirty years was my sister Salina, and I had abandoned her. "I'm not worthy of being loved."

"Yes, you are. Preserving life—celebrating it—is so much more satisfying than taking it. They taught you to close your heart to people...you were forbidden to form attachments to anyone. Now you will have the chance to love, and be loved in return. It's a chance you deserve—your sacrifice has earned it. Now you must stay alive, so you can take it."

I wanted to see her, to touch her hair...to comfort her. I struggled, trying to free myself from the wretched animal, to no avail. Darkness roared in my ears, and drew a black curtain over my eyes. I neither saw Fythia nor heard her gentle voice again.

***

I would like to tell you that all the bad dreams went away after that, but I can't. In fact, I spent several weeks in various states of wakefulness. I was unconscious for the most part. No one came to visit me in my dreams, for which I was mostly thankful, but I heard their voices as I had heard them before.

You did this! You took me from my wife and children! You didn't even know me!

Yes, I did. It was wrong, and I'm sorry. I will never take a life again on the bidding of another.

No, none of you is ever guilty...

Yes we are. I am. No one bears this burden but me.

He held on to his humanity—to the things his father taught him. Didn't your father teach you that it's wrong to kill?

Of course he did. Please stop! Leave me in peace.

It would be quite some time before that peace would come. I was dimly aware of being lashed to a horse-drawn sledge, being dragged over the sandy ground, and being in a great deal of pain. I heard voices, but didn't recognize any of them. I remember being given water. I tasted blood sometimes, and that would shock me awake for a few moments, just long enough to view the stars.

Then I woke up in a room bathed in fire-light, and I knew I might actually have a real chance of living. A woman held a water-vessel to my lips, speaking soft words in a tongue I knew well. Her eyes—glorious, dark brown, and filled with intelligence—held no judgment of me.

"What's your name?" she asked, gently cleaning the sweat from my forehead.

I didn't know whether I could speak. *And what should I tell her? I have forsaken the man who was Beltran, and I'm not worthy of Glennroy—the brave boy who protected his sister.*

"My name is...El-morah," I whispered.

She threw her head back, tossing long, soft black hair across one shoulder. I caught the wonderful scent of a young woman unmarred by sickness, heard the laughter of a free spirit unfettered by guilt. "My name," she said, "is Mohani."

Mohani. The name means "beautiful." Never has a woman been named so well. As I looked into her eyes again, her clear gaze reflecting the purity of her spirit, my eyes filled with tears of shame. She thoughtfully dabbed them away.

"Well, El-morah, I think you're going to live," she said.

I was going to live. Not just exist, but truly *live*. I raised my right hand from the coverlet, and she took it, as if to lead me out of the shadows. I had been given another chance.

"The Wheel turns," she said, smiling down at me.

El-morah's tale continues in The Elfhunter Trilogy...

BOOK LIST

Tales of Alterra (The Elfhunter Trilogy)
Elfhunter
Fire-heart
Ravenshade

Alterra Histories
The Fire King
Fallen Embers
The Shadow-man

Undiscovered Realms
Outcaste (2015)

ABOUT C.S. MARKS

C.S. Marks has often been described as a Renaissance woman. The daughter of academic parents, she holds a Ph.D. in Biology and has spent the past two decades teaching Biology and Equine Science. She is currently a Full Professor at Saint Mary-of-the-Woods College in west central Indiana.

She began writing shortly after the untimely death of her father, who was a Professor of American Literature at Butler University. A gifted artist, musician, and songwriter, she plays and sings Celtic music. She enjoys archery, and makes hand-crafted longbows using primitive tools.

Horses are her passion, and she is an accomplished horsewoman, having competed in the sport of endurance racing for many years. One of only a handful of Americans to complete the prestigious Tom Quilty Australian national championship hundred-mile ride, she has described this moment as her finest hour.

She and her husband, Jeff, share their home with ten dogs (predominantly Welsh Corgis) and five horses. They live deep in the forest, where there are miles and miles of trail riding to be had.

WHERE TO FIND C.S. MARKS

The Author's Website: CSMarks.com

Facebook.com/Alterra.CSMarks

Twitter.com/CSMarks_Alterra

Stay up to date with what's happening with C.S. Marks by joining the mailing list. You will receive exclusive teasers and be the first to know when a new book as been released.

Sign Up For the C.S. Marks Mailing List at CSMarks.com

Made in the USA
Lexington, KY
14 July 2017